ALSO BY CHRIS DiLEO

Hudson House
Calamity
Blood Mountain
Meat Camp (with Scott Nicholson)
The Devil Virus
Dead End
Dark Heart
Revival Road

CHILDREN OF FIRE

CHRIS DiLEO

BLEEDING EDGE BOOKS

CHILDREN OF FIRE
Copyright © 2022 by Chris DiLeo
All Rights Reserved

ISBN: 979-8218050344
Cover artwork by Don Noble | Rooster Republic Press
Book design & formatting by Todd Keisling | Dullington Design Co.

This is a work of fiction. Names, characters, businesses, places, events, and incidents are either the products of the authors' imaginations or used in a fictitious manner. Any resemblance to actual persons, living or dead, or actual events is purely coincidental.

No part of this publication may be reproduced, stored in a retrieval system, or transmitted in any form or by any means, without the prior permission in writing of the publisher, nor be otherwise circulated in any form of binding or cover than that in which it is published and without a similar condition including this condition being imposed on the subsequent purchaser.

Bleeding Edge Books
www.bleedingedgepub.com

For Jenn

"I baptize you with water, but one who is more powerful than I will come... [and] He will baptize you with the Holy Spirit and with fire."

Luke 3:16

PART ONE

1

I used to think being a cop and a detective gave my life purpose.

You go into law enforcement, I know I did, because you want to help people. Cops get a bad rap because of course there's bad cops—cowboys who want to be tough guys, who want to intimidate the vulnerable and push around the weak, beat up anyone who gives them a hard time, anyone who doesn't immediately respect the badge and the gun.

Some of those guys are dicks and some are major dicks. Unfortunately, some of them still manage pretty good police work. I'm not forgiving them; those guys who shake down a crack addict or filch from Evidence or plant it at the scene. Especially the Chauvins of the world, who think a knee-on-the-neck-until-dead is SOP. They should all be given their well-earned punishment.

I'm only saying life isn't always black and white. Sometimes bad cops make good and good cops go bad. Most of the time cops, like everybody else, are a mix of the two. Always in flux.

My point, if I have one, is that even when I thought working cases gave my life meaning, I was full of shit and didn't know it.

2

I didn't grab the gun I keep in my nightstand when knocks thundered on my apartment door, but I did consider it. I'm not paranoid (and I'm not being hunted or in trouble with the law or the mob), but I live in a basement apartment, have an unlisted number, never have guests, and if you didn't know better you'd think my place was unoccupied.

Maybe I am a *little* paranoid.

Police work will do that to you.

"Yeah, look," I said cutting off a trio of knocks. "I don't have my gun on me but if you're here to kill me let me know so I can go get it."

"Sorry," a guy on the other side of the door said. "It's me, Brock."

I'll admit it took a moment. It's an unusual name, Brock, so you'd expect to remember if you met one, but I blanked—for a second, anyway.

Therapists call that selective memory.

"If you're looking for marriage advice, you should try somewhere else."

"I need your help. *Please.*"

My next zinger, something about the virtues of staying single, died the moment I opened the door.

Rumpled dress shirt, untucked, stubble-beard, eyes red and oily, Brock looked like shit, but he was on High Alert, back rigid, shoulders tensed.

"Rowe," he said. That's my last name. No one ever calls me by my first, Landon. "It's about Melissa. I need your help."

I almost made the crack about marriage advice again, but five years as a cop and ten as a detective taught me who to press and how, and the way Brock looked, even a little humor might push him over the edge.

"Beer?" I asked.

His eyes went big as if that were insane.

"No," he said coming into the room.

"Sit down, tell me what's up."

He walked directly into the coffee table, rattling the empty beer bottles I'd left there from the last few nights, looked from the black leather couch (what Melissa called my 'bachelor couch') to the La-Z-Boy recliner that was so worn the wood edges protruded from the armrests and on which my cat, Sherman, was sleeping in a perfect curl of orange fur.

"Look," he said, "I don't know everything that happened between you and Melissa but I get that she can be flighty."

"Stuck with you a while, though, didn't she? What is it, eight years? Ten?"

"It's only been four," Brock said.

"Feels like ages ago to me. Barely remember it."

"I'm not here for a pissing contest, Rowe."

"Shame. I got a full bladder."

"I'm serious."

"So am I. Those beers don't drink themselves."

Brock looked around. He made a sound somewhere between a sigh and a chuckle.

At over six-feet tall, he had height, reach, and weight on me, but he was a history teacher or something, while I was trained in the army how to kill a man with my bare hands if need be. Besides, I also had a gun.

"It's not as if I want to be here," he said.

"Makes two of us."

"I'll get to it."

"Please. I haven't even had my coffee yet."

"It's almost noon."

"Your point?"

I could keep being a prick and typically I would (I'm not sure if I enjoyed it too much or no longer knew how to be any other way, Melissa might answer that better than I could), but I managed to pull the reins in and ask him why the hell he was here.

"Melissa's gone."

"Up and left, huh? No surprise. Take it from me, some of those retreats can go for a week or two. Or longer. She once did a ten-day fast at some Buddhist temple where supposedly no one spoke, either. You meditate *silently* for ten days while you starve yourself. Sounds like bullshit to me. I can shut up *and* not eat right here."

"Rowe—"

"Though I would've loved watching Melissa try to stay mute. You know what I mean. She gives a running narrative of her every thought."

"Rowe—"

"Maybe it doesn't bother you. Yet. It will. Enjoy the peace and quiet because once she's back—"

"Rowe!"

I stopped.

"She's not at a retreat. I know where she is. She took our kid and joined some religious commune or something."

I wasn't at a loss for asshole comments to make, but the worry on Brock's face finally kept me quiet. He looked like he might start sobbing.

"I need you to help me get my kid back. *Please.*"

3

I got him to sit down and Sherman immediately abandoned the recliner for a human lap. I offered a beer again but Brock shook his head. I left his open on the coffee table while I swigged from my own and sat on a swirl of cat fur on the recliner.

"Tell me," I said.

Five days ago, Brock came home to find Melissa's phone on the kitchen counter and a simple handwritten note beneath. *Don't try to find us. I know what I'm doing.*

"At least she left a note," Brock said, and I was thinking the same thing. When you marry a woman who's flighty, you can't expect she'll always tell you when she's going to fly. "Didn't take her car or tell her mom anything about leaving. She just left. Barely took any clothes. Her phone was reset back to factory settings. Everything deleted."

I had questions, but only one mattered.

"Where'd she go?"

Elbows on his thighs, head bowed, he was mumbling to himself. Something about trying harder or how he thought she'd been doing better and then he was saying his kid's name over and over, punctuated with curses.

If I were working in an official capacity, I might let him ramble among his thoughts for a while and then go over the whole story—several times—fleshing out details, identifying inconsistencies, building a case, or at least the context of a case, but I cut him off.

I couldn't stand hearing him say his kid's name.

"Brock, *stop.*"

He looked at me with watery eyes. But there was rage there, too, and that I understood.

All too well, you could say.

"Where is Melissa?"

"She's three hours from here going west. South of Rochester in some random town." He sounded calmer, focused. When someone's in a panic, you ask them questions they can answer. You don't ever tell them to relax. Doesn't work. I know that from experience, professionally and personally.

4

I brewed coffee, black and muddy. He only sipped it but it gave him something to do—keeping both hands on the mug, his knuckles chafed raw, taking mid-sentence sips—while I questioned him for more details. The name of the town was Tabes. It's so small you can't find it on most New York maps. When he started blabbering about how he should've seen this coming, I cut him off. I didn't need, nor want, the whole story. I wasn't a detective anymore, not even the beat cop I was before that, so I cut through the extraneous shit and got right to it.

"How long before you called the police?"

"I never thought she'd take our son."

I thought of charred photo albums.

"How many times you call before the police took you seriously?"

"I had to go there, and after they made me sit and wait

for almost two hours, they sent me to the Staties. And they made me wait another hour before someone would hear me out."

He gave me a look that seemed to suggest I'd probably done the same to untold numbers of distraught people who just wanted the police to help them. Or maybe I was "projecting," as they say, because of course I had done that.

"What'd they say, the Staties?"

"They went there, knew exactly the place and the people." Another sip. Something wanted to break on his face but he kept himself together. "They found her. Spoke with her. Said she's there voluntarily. Called it a 'mental health escape' or something."

"And your kid, Ethan?"

He stared at me.

Blood splashed inside my chest.

"Eli," I said. "Sorry."

Brock started to sip more coffee and stopped. Even with both hands on it, the mug was shaking. "She told them she didn't have any children. She told them"—his voice was breaking, either toward grief or rage—"her child was dead."

I couldn't stop myself. It slipped out.

"Bitch," I said.

5

Melissa and I had a boy. Ethan.
He didn't survive.
Neither did our marriage.

6

made sure they actually spoke with her," Brock said. "Made them stare at several pictures of her and confirm that's who they spoke to."

"That's good," I said, thinking it was also paranoid and insulting.

"I'm not an idiot, you know," he said. "I watch crime shows and read too."

"Right." Behind him was my collection of dogeared paperbacks. Cobens and Korytas and Connellys and Childs and Winslows. Melissa called it my Boys Can Read Too collection. Wedged among them were books on police and detective work, true crime books, and a slender photo album with charred pages.

"Made them look at a picture of Eli, too. You know what they said?"

I waited, although I could guess.

"They hadn't even *looked* for him. They accepted

what Melissa told them. As if I'd made up that we had a child together."

Some men will do anything to get their women back, I thought.

"So, I called the FBI."

I smirked but not because he shouldn't have done it. Books and movies make calling the FBI look easy as ordering a pizza. Somebody's missing? Pick up a phone and CUT TO: a pair of agents in suits or maybe windbreakers with FBI emblazoned on the back knocking on doors or swinging flashlight beams through dark, rainy woods.

I held up a hand. "They love going after religious cults, practically a favorite pastime of theirs, but you can't just call them or go to HQ. They don't take direction from civilians. Or former detectives."

I knew what he was thinking. Rowe must know somebody in the Bureau who can get an investigation started. I did—I have contacts in the FBI, the CIA, ATF, and in local jurisdictions through the Hudson Valley and beyond, but many of those bridges had been burned. Or were at least in disrepair. Still, though, I was good at talking to other authorities. I spoke their language, which is more about attitude than vernacular, and I could get people to help me out. If I wanted.

"You were married to her," Brock said. "You know how she thinks."

"I think she's going to come back. Could be in a week, a month—could be tomorrow. You've been married to her long enough to know that."

Some people call it "being flighty" and I've heard it called "getting rabbit in your blood" or "lighting out for the territories," but for Melissa it was "going on a soul quest."

Why all the retreats? I once asked her. *Why the aimless hikes?*

I'm on a soul quest, she said.

Those "soul quests" became something more fanatical and desperate after the fire.

"You still on Castle Terrace?"

He knew what I was really asking.

"Yes."

"Maybe that's part of the problem," I said.

There was no reason to say that, of course. He really wasn't an idiot, but I really am an asshole and hard as you might try you can't change your nature.

"I get what you're saying about Melissa, but I'm here because of my kid. I want him back. I want him safe. I'm sure you can understand that."

If we really were having a pissing contest, Brock would've just won.

"Yeah, I can understand that."

"You'll help?"

I sipped my coffee, spat it back in the cup, and stood.

"Is that a yes?"

"I'm switching back to beer."

7

I asked if Melissa had been especially strange lately or simply "Melissa strange." He said he hadn't noticed anything. That might be true or at least he thought it was true, but our minds pick up all kinds of things that we don't want to acknowledge.

I asked him who picked her up. He didn't know.

I asked exactly what she took with her. He said he didn't take an inventory.

I asked if he had the note she left.

"None of this matters," Brock said. Sherman leaped off his lap and bolted out of the room. "I know where she is. Where my son is."

I gulped a few swallows of beer. "If you want someone to snatch your kid back, I got a guy'll do it for a reasonable price. But if you want my help, you have to let me do things my way."

He was leaning forward as if readying to pounce.

I waited.

"Okay, fine," he said, body sagging. "Whatever you want, but can we please go there tonight?"

Another gulp. My mouth felt swollen.

"I go alone."

"What? No. She's going to lose her shit if she sees you."

One more gulp. "I'll get the number of that guy for you."

He let me get to the doorway before getting to his feet and saying my name. In the kitchen beyond, Sherman sat near his empty food bowl and eyed me with certain conviction.

"Fine, you go alone. But I want you to call me once you know anything."

"I'll call you when I have your kid."

"Okay. Now what?"

"How has Mel handled COVID?"

I could guess, but I wanted to hear it from him.

"Not well."

Did that mean her usual crying fits and vacant stares or had she progressed to something worse?

Brock did not elaborate.

"You have the note?"

"No."

"What was it written on?"

"What? I don't know."

"Brock, listen to me. I'm going to feed my cat because he's giving me the death stare, but when I come back, you're going to tell me what I want. I know what I'm doing. I'm asking you questions you know the answers to. You just need to take a minute and think about it."

I gave Sherman a can of organic shredded chicken (his food was more expensive, and healthier, than mine), a few gentle head caresses he tolerated, and when I returned to the living room Brock hadn't moved but his face had changed.

He'd been thinking.

"Her note was on the back of a prayer card."

8

"There was a priest," Brock said. "Melissa used to talk about him. I thought they were having an affair, but she said the guy's almost sixty. Who knows? Daddy issues, right?"

"He's sixty-two," I said. "Father Benjamin Reed. Benny. I call him Benny Boy. He doesn't like that. You're right, though. She's spent most of her life looking for a replacement father figure. I was one. You're one. Benny Boy's another."

"You think he has something to do with this?"

"Maybe."

I was done with both coffee and beer, but I wished I were still a smoker. Dragging on a cigarette is always good for filling the pauses in a conversation.

"What else do you need to know?"

"Give me the exact location of this... retreat."

"It's not some yoga place or Buddhist meditation or whatever," Brock said. "I think it's a cult. A *real* cult."

We exchanged numbers and he texted me the address.

"Go home," I said and heard my voice getting a little tight on that word "home." Why the hell had she stayed there after what happened? *Because she's a masochist,* I thought. *Why else would she have married me?*

"Rowe?"

"Go. This shouldn't take long."

PART TWO

9

Father Benjamin Reed lived in a brown ranch-style house in the old part of a housing development. A smear of asphalt, looking like a swollen scar, divided the grey-and-crumbling old from the... well, less-old part. Benny Boy's house was on the crumbling side where the ground sloped downwards. A rusty beater of a station wagon was parked in the driveway. Untrimmed bushes obscured windows.

I knocked and waited. Knocked some more, louder, and then rode the bell for almost fifteen seconds before he opened the door.

He was huffing, face blanched and sweaty. A cloth face mask with a cross on it sagged off his nose.

He hesitated at the threshold, staring wide-eyed.

"Thought you were dead," I said. "Almost had to break in."

"Landon?"

"Scared of something?" I asked.

He flinched and I thought he might drop back and shut the door but then he removed his mask and said he'd been praying.

"Sorry to interrupt. Long time, Benny Boy."

He did a good job hiding his annoyance at the nickname, coming out fully onto the porch as I made room for him, and shutting the door and squinting up at my truck, a beat-up Ford that always threatens to die but never does. He shielded his eyes from the sun with one hand like he was kid asking a question in class.

I stopped so he'd have to stay in that position, a skinny shadow slashing across his face.

"You could've called," he said. "I wasn't expecting visitors."

"Won't be but a minute. Then you can go back to praying."

"Okay." He shifted his feet. They were bare. His khakis were loose and his over-starched button-down cut boxy angles around him. A white cross was stitched on the breast pocket. He was freshly shaved and what hair he had gleamed wet.

"When was the last time you saw Melissa?" I asked. I was in a work shirt, jeans, and my ancient Red Wing work boots. Same thing I wore as a detective. Back then, everyone was always asking me where the construction site was.

He glanced at the street and back at me. "Aren't you two divorced?"

"You know we are, Benny Boy."

"Why are you looking for her?"

"When did you last see her?"

Another street-glance. "Few days ago."

"As in three? Or was it five? Maybe less, maybe more?"

He considered. "Thought you left the force."

"I did."

"Violent tendencies, wasn't it?"

"Irreconcilable differences," I said. "Same as my divorce."

This time, he checked farther down the street, losing the shadow on his face and making him squint, which brought out the wrinkles around his eyes and those on his forehead.

"Expecting someone?"

"What? No."

"There's no cavalry coming. Just me."

"Local kids been playing pranks," he said.

"Oh? Like what?"

"What?"

"What sort of pranks?"

"What is it you want, Landon?"

From the breast pocket of my gray work shirt, I tugged out a memo book and a pen. I opened it and scanned my notes. It was a mix of grocery items (cat food, olive oil, bread), reminders (check leak under bathroom sink), and a messy sketch of Sherman I scribbled when drunk.

"Ah, yes, here it is—when did you last see Melissa?"

Benny Boy stared at me.

"My sport coat's in the truck," I said, "if you want me to get fully into character."

He hesitated and said, "I haven't seen her in a while."

"You said a few days ago."

"I misspoke."

"Okay. How long's a while?"

I readied my pen as if awaiting some vital piece of information. In reality, the answer was irrelevant. What mattered was why he wasn't being straight about it.

"Has something happened to her?"

"It's a simple question, Benny Boy."

"You're accusing me of something." Another street-glance.

"Should I?"

His shoulder finally gave out from keeping his hand raised against the light and he dropped his arm. He was sifting through thoughts in his head. Selecting the best response.

Told you I was a bit paranoid.

"I need to be understanding," he said and turned toward me. No squinting this time. "It's been… six years? It happened in August, didn't it? The anniversary must be close. You're hurting. You don't like me, I understand. I was only trying to help."

I thought of the gun in my glove compartment, and of the tool bag on the passenger seat. Specifically of the Estwing bricklayer's hammer inside that bag.

Father Reed took tentative steps toward me. He held his hands before him, palms-up. "I know you don't want to hear this, but God loves you. All of you. He forgives you of your sins. He forgives how you failed your marriage vows. He forgives how you failed your work obligations. He forgives you for not protecting your son, and He wants you to know that Ethan is with Him and—"

He didn't get the rest out because I grabbed him, lifting him off his feet, and I shoved him hard against his front door, pressing him there with my left forearm across his throat. My short sleeve pulled up enough for him to see the tattoo stretching onto my shoulder. From his angle, it might look like two large ink blots, but he knew what it was: my son's feet.

"Here's how this is going to work, Benny Boy," I said, inches from his face. He squirmed, cheeks turning red, his breathing sharp and thin. "I need some very simple answers from you. Tell me what I want to know, and I'll go. Keep screwing around, and this can get a lot more uncomfortable. You're hiding something, and I don't know what it is, but you better come clean right now. If you do, I'll play nice, I promise." He stopped squirming. Surrendered. His eyes were huge, his skin purpling. I let up on his throat and then immediately pressed harder so he couldn't breathe at all. "And if you say one more thing about my son, all bets are off. *Got it?*"

"Please," he wheezed.

I released him. He almost fell over, heaving for air.

"Inside," I said. *"Now."*

10

The house was a holdover from the seventies and had not been updated since. Walls of cheap wood paneling and beaten brown carpet coupled with thick curtains nearly drawn to a close across the front window made the place into a cave. It smelled stale.

He stumbled several feet down the hall toward the kitchen, bare feet tracking across carpet.

"Stop," I said, shutting the door behind me.

He kept going, wheezing and coughing.

"Stay back. I'm not vaccinated."

I chuckled. "Sorry, my mask's in the truck. But I'm sure God'll protect you."

He was still moving, almost at the kitchen. Maybe he just wanted a drink of water. Or maybe he was thinking of grabbing a knife.

"*Stop,*" I said again.

He did, slumped in the kitchen doorway, diffused sunlight catching swirls of dust around his head.

The floor creaked beneath my boots. "I don't trust you," I said.

He tried to speak and suffered a coughing fit instead.

Dish towels with crosses on them hung off the sink in which plates and glasses waited to be cleaned. A fly buzzed somewhere. I didn't see any knives. I smelled the acrid aroma of burned bacon.

"Stand up straight," I said.

If he were a different type of man, he'd take the opportunity to sucker-punch me in the gut. He was a slimy fool, but he wasn't a complete idiot and definitely not a brawler.

"Please," he said again, sounding better and leaning against the doorway frame. "I'll tell you whatever you want."

"Last time you saw Melissa?"

"Five days ago."

I gestured for him to elaborate.

"She came here, didn't stay long."

"What'd you talk about?"

"Faith and hope."

I let go a dismissive snort.

"Where'd she go?"

"I need to... to sit down."

I grabbed him. "Where'd she go?"

He sniffed as if he had a runny nose.

"There's something you need to see," he said.

11

In the living room, he had a floor-model TV that might be forty years old and a VHS player nearly as ancient.

A gold crucifix hung on the wall above the TV.

Benny Boy searched through a wooden crate that resembled a pirate's treasure chest. I heard VHS tapes tumbling against each other.

"This," he said, holding up a tape in a clear plastic case, "is what I want to show you."

"Home video? You know, you can have those converted to DVDs now. Easy as a trip to Walmart."

"I can't do that."

"Is it a sex tape, Benny Boy?"

Instead of responding, he opened the plastic case, removed the VHS cassette (I couldn't catch what was scrawled on the white sticker), and loaded it into the player. He turned on the TV, put it to channel 3, and stepped back.

We stood over it, staring down as the black-and-white

static changed to a skipping, bouncing image with distorted lines rolling up the screen.

"No popcorn?" I asked.

A lush mountain fills the screen. The time stamp at the bottom: July 16, 1999. Over twenty years ago. I'd just graduated high school.

The image is steady for a few seconds and then cuts to a wobbling gait as the person holding the camera moves through the woods. A path through tall grass leads to a thick canopy of trees as the camera moves beneath them. Something familiar about this.

"You may recognize the location," Benny said.

I didn't say anything but I didn't have to wonder long.

The crunch of gravel and dirt beneath the camera person's feet changes to the scrape of solid rock. The trees and the tall grasses disappear as a gray sky fills the screen.

"Okay," someone off screen says. "Here's perfect."

The image tilts down from the cloudy sky to reveal a large smooth outcropping of rock that slants upward.

"Lake Minnewaska," I said.

Benny didn't need to confirm I was right.

The camera stands still and, from behind the shot there emerges a lanky man with hair down past his shoulders. He wears jeans and a faded tee-shirt. He walks straight across the rock outcropping to the cliff edge where rock meets sky, and turns. A bandanna keeps his hair off his face. His feet are bare.

"This," he says, arms out at his sides, "is glorious."

With the gray behind him, he looks like he's floating there. Crucified against the sky.

The man gestures for the cameraperson to come closer.

The rock falls away into an expansive vista I'd seen in person a few times. This was shot on Gertrude's Nose, one of the most popular trails at Lake Minnewaska, part of the Shawangunk Mountains, what locals call the Gunks. Thousands of people trekked it yearly.

The image on the video is a reminder why.

When you stand where the camera person stands, the Hudson River Valley stretches for miles and miles beneath you. There are trees as far as you can see cut up by distant farmland and slices of backroads. It is a valley of trees both evergreen and those beginning to change to yellow and gold and brown that reaches all the way to the Catskill Mountains in the distance, so far off they look like faded images, ghost mountains, something from a fantasy story where good-hearted heroes go on a quest to defeat evil.

From that view on Gertrude's Nose, you might believe in God.

Or think you are one.

"This is the Lord's country," the man says. His grin is youthful sincerity with a touch of smugness. I figure he's twenty-five at the most.

The camera moves in close. The man's face fills the screen.

His dark eyes are like polished black stones. Then he steps aside and the video gives us that glorious view again. Out on the prow-like tip—the jutting rock of Gertrude's Nose—it might be a thousand-foot drop or more to the rocks and trees below.

"Time to cleanse us of our sins," he says off camera.

Blades of bright sunlight slice through the ceiling of clouds as if on cue.

Even on this VHS-quality tape, the sunlight is startlingly bright and magnificent.

"Just look at that," the man says. "We're all so blessed."

The image zooms toward that light and holds, taking it all in.

Benny nodded at the screen. "Eamon Fischer," he said with a distinct note of awe.

"Friend of yours?"

"We traveled in similar circles."

"A group of wannabe cult leaders?"

On the TV, the picture cuts to a close-up of a used campfire site, ash and dirt strewn together inside a circle of rocks scorched black from the licks of open flames. Then sticks and dry twigs are dropped onto the dirt and a pair of hands, the man's no doubt, form a kindling teepee. A match lights off camera and then the flame comes into view.

"You know anything about the earliest Christians?" Benny asked.

"You mean when Jesus supposedly walked the Earth?"

"There were many who didn't believe," Benny said. "Most, in fact, believed that the sect of Jews who chose to follow the word of this mysterious man, Jesus, were fools. They were being misled. Tricked. You could say the beginning of Christianity was viewed as little more than a cult."

I nodded as if in agreement. "And look how far they've come in two thousand years," I said. "Just takes a few Crusades and a few million deaths to make your cult a real religion."

On the video, the kindling is quickly catching fire.

"The Christians were persecuted—"

"Please don't regale me with tales of them being fed to lions."

The fire on the screen is going well now, and when the man's hands come back into view, they hold a small piece of paper. On it in large uneven letters is the word PRIDE.

"My sin," Eamon Fischer says. "I hereby cleanse myself of pride."

He crumples the paper, hesitates, and reaches out to set the paper ball atop the teepee where the flames stretch all around his hand.

He doesn't flinch.

The paper catches fire and burns quickly.

"Praise be the Lord," Fischer says.

A moment later, a different set of hands come into view,

they might be a woman's. Her paper says SELFISHNESS. She crumples it, places it on the fire.

"Oh," I said, "please tell me it goes on like this for the rest of the tape. What's next, gluttony? Sloth? Please tell me someone wrote lust."

On the video, another set of hands and another piece of paper. The word this time is DISBELIEF. Off camera, Eamon Fischer is invoking the name of God in some prayer or benediction that might be real or made-up. It's difficult to tell the difference, at least that's what I think. The few times I've been to church, including my own son's funeral, the prayers always made me think of a poorly performed school play in which there's a script but no one really knows how to deliver their lines, or what the point of the whole thing is.

As another set of hands appears, Benny Boy squats and hits FF. The footage of more hands and more paper crumpling and burning goes by in a quickening blur as squiggly lines crease the image.

"Please tell me there's more."

"I'm trying to make a point," Benny said.

"I'm not in the mood for subtlety."

"You never have been."

"Cute. So, what's the point?"

"You were a detective. Put two and two together."

"Melissa is with him, I get that. She's going to write her sins on pieces of paper and watch them burn. That'll cure her, right? You want me to guess what the sins are? Selfishness is a good one. Bitchiness, maybe. How about *irresponsibility*? That works."

Without turning from the fast-forwarding images on the TV, Benny gave me what could be a rehearsed spiel.

"Some people think the Hudson Valley and the surrounding area *is* the Holy Land. We have Christians, and Jews, and Muslims, of course. But we have the Hasidics who have almost taken over Monroe and the Chinese Buddhists at Dragon Springs in Cuddebackville and we're now the world center for Jehovah's Witnesses in Newburgh. While everyone focuses on Israelis and Palestinians killing each other over lifeless desert, we are here in a genuine fertile crescent of Eden."

"Wow," I said. "And I've lived here my whole life and never knew."

"New York was even the home to the Church of the Latter-day Saints. The Mormons."

"Until New Yorkers drove them out."

"Precisely."

"Which is what happened to your buddy on the video here?"

"In a manner of speaking." Benny plucked at his face mask. "Eamon Fischer is a genuine man of God and could've been an excellent priest at any parish, in *any* faith, but just as the Jews didn't believe the earliest Christians, and yes, just as the Pharaohs had those Christians fed to the lions, the locals drove him out. We always fear the outsider, the different one, the man who dares to believe in something other, something *grander*."

I pretended to ponder that.

"Or maybe New Yorkers aren't so easily duped," I said. "This footage is 22 years old. This Fischer guy still burning sins?"

"Ah," Benny said and hit PLAY. "Here. Watch."

The camera is set farther back so the fire, still burning, is farther away and you can now see a group of people sitting crosslegged around it. Directly ahead on the other side of the fire sits Eamon Fischer. The flames almost reach his chin, and the light makes his face glow.

Mr. Holy Man, I thought.

Fischer raises his hands, palms up, the universal welcoming gesture. "The power of God flows through me as it flows through each one of us and through all that surrounds us."

"Please tell me they're going to strip naked and dance in the woods," I said.

"One at a time," Fischer says, "we shall heal each other and know God's glory."

Someone stands up directly in front of the camera, blocking the entire image a moment before moving around the fire toward Fischer. The man is barefoot. He gets to his knees beside Fischer, who tells him to remove his shirt. The man does so. The lighting is poor so it's difficult to see the man clearly but it's easy to see pale flesh so near to flickering flames.

I wanted to make a sarcastic comment but I was afraid my remark about the burning power of faith might actually be what I was about to witness.

Fischer turns to face the man. "Do you accept the Lord into your entire being, into your heart and soul?"

"Yes," the man says.

"Shit," I said, recognizing the voice.

Fischer places a hand on the man's head. "The power of God is the power of galaxies. The power of infinity. That power is within you. Let it show you the way."

There is a pause as Fischer reaches for something with his other hand. Something near the fire.

For a moment, it appears as if a glowing hot ember of fire floats before Fischer's face before it's clear he's holding a metal rod like a fire poker but with something burning at the end.

A branding iron.

"The Lord be with you," Fischer says.

"And also with you," the man says.

Then Fischer presses the burning end of the branding iron directly onto the center of the man's chest.

Flesh sizzles.

The man screams.

But he doesn't move, doesn't recoil, doesn't yell for it to stop.

It's only a moment, but feels much longer.

What the hell am I watching?

The man's scream is not one of pain so much as one of pure adrenaline.

Fischer removes the iron, setting it back in the fire, and the two men embrace like long-lost relatives who've finally found each other. Other voices cry out "Praise God!"

Benny pressed STOP and the TV went black.

The air had thickened in here and I felt warm.

"Must've hurt," I said.

Benny stared.

"Show me," I said.

He undid several buttons on his shirt and tugged down his undershirt: a cross was singed into the center of his chest.

12

The long-ago burned skin was in the middle of a swirl of gray hair. His flesh was thin and wrinkly, but around the raised scar of the branded cross it was tight and angry red.

"Leave Melissa where she is, Landon," he said. "Eamon will keep her safe. He'll show her the way."

"And burn her chest with a fucking cross?"

Slowly, he buttoned his shirt. "You know why I showed you that?"

"Because you're insane?"

He sighed. "Because Eamon Fischer is a good man. A man of God."

"Who burned a cross into your chest."

"Not much different from a tattoo," he said.

"Actually, it's a lot different. It's fucking fire melting skin."

"It's an act of purification. We are all children of fire."

"Funny, I always thought fire was the Devil's thing. You sure you're worshipping the right guy?"

"I was dying," Benny said. "In April of 1999, I was diagnosed with Stage 4 prostate cancer. I was barely forty, but it happens."

"You expect me to believe this Fischer guy healed you?"

"Belief is what it's all about."

"You mean, self-delusion."

Instead of getting a rise out of Benny, my comments made him nod his head. "You think you're smarter than everyone, Landon. Most non-believers credit their lack of belief to their intelligence. People who believe in an almighty power must be stupid, right?"

"You said it."

Benny picked at his face mask again. I wanted to rip it off and breathe hot air right onto him.

"I'm not going to tell you where they are unless you agree to respect the power of belief."

I laughed. "I know where they are. Melissa's husband knew *exactly* where she went."

"Then why did you come here?"

"I wanted to know what you know, and I wanted some idea what I was walking into. It's not Mel I'm looking for, anyway. Her husband wants their son back."

Benny swallowed. "She didn't have her son with her."

"You're sure?"

"Yes."

"Maybe he was outside. She take an Uber? Borrow someone's car?"

He shook his head. "I drove her to Fischer."

"Of course you did."

"I drove her but it was—"

"Oh, yes, God. It was God who led her there. You had nothing to do with it."

"I'm merely His instrument."

"Why aren't you with him? Why live in a community among us heathens when you could be in the wilderness with the man who scorched your flesh?"

"God has a plan for each of us. There are demands set upon each soul. Sacrifices to be made. The crosses we carry can be very heavy."

I held up my hand. "Sorry. Don't care."

"Would you like to pray? Years ago, I converted my basement into a sort of home church." He gestured back toward the hall.

"I'll pass. Be seeing you, Benny Boy."

PART THREE

13

It's a three-hour drive, but I made it in under two-and-a-half.

Route 17 zigzags west out of Orange County into Sullivan and out past Binghamton and keeps going west through Elmira and Corning, which is where Route 86 slopes north and becomes 390 toward Rochester. Just east of Rochester is Palmyra, the birthplace of the Latter-day Saints.

I almost missed the green highway sign for Tabes, NY. I was somewhere north of Dansville and south of Geneseo.

The exit road brought me out to a back country road where an ancient sign for GAS hung warped and crooked.

At the gas station, which had only two pumps outside and a store with yellowing flyers plastered on the windows and cases of dusty bottled water stacked in the direct sun, I filled my tank and grabbed a bag of nuts and a bottle of plain seltzer.

The guy working the register, presumably the only

employee, as well as the only person in the place, looked like he'd been baked for two hours at 400°.

He squinted at me through tan, wrinkled folds. "You're in law enforcement?"

"What makes you think that?"

"Had a brother who was a trooper," he said. "All you guys get that same look."

"Oh, yeah? What's the look?"

He took my ten dollar bill and handed me the change.

"Like you're expecting something bad'll happen."

"My ex-wife would agree with you."

The man made a sound that meant he understood, and then said he had an ex-wife somewhere and he could tell me some stories about what she would say if I wanted to hear them.

"Actually," I said, "I'd love to hear anything you know about a man named Eamon Fischer. He's a priest, or at least calls himself one, and might be living in the woods around here."

The old guy was nodding. He leaned on the register, as if settling in for a conversation. With the cigarettes stacked behind him (a thing I've heard called the "Tobacco Power Wall"), it looked like an old magazine ad where grizzled men smoked because that's what tough guys did.

"Oh, yeah, I know who you mean," he said. "Never met him, but we all know about *them*, the Children of Fire."

My eyebrows went up.

"Yup, that's what they call themselves. When word got around about that, the Town Board tried to have them driven out for 'sacrilegious abomination.' No one came right out and called them Devil Worshippers, but everyone was thinking it. Didn't work. One call from some civil liberties lawyer and that was that. They rented the land. They have a permit for occupancy *and* burning. Nothing we can do."

Now I made a sound of agreeable commiseration. "You think they're Satanists?"

"I'm nobody's saint," he said, "but I also don't live among the animals and dance around burning fires."

"Any idea how many of them there are?"

"Could be two or three dozen, last I heard. They light some big fires, I'll tell you that. Fire department had to go over not once but three times. Not that they could get the truck back there. Even tried making a new road to get there. Graham, he's the Fire Chief, speaks at every Town Board meeting, trying to get rid of them."

"You know where they are?"

"Sure. They're not hiding. It's a mile or two up the road." He gestured. "You'll see a wooden sign they put up."

I thanked him for his time and then bought a pack of Marlboro Reds and a bright yellow pocket lighter.

At the door, I looked back at him. "You said you *had* a brother who was a trooper. What happened to him?"

"Died."

"Line of duty?"

The old guy took a breath and gave me a rueful smile. "House fire."

"No, shit," I said.

14

Ethan was in his crib when the fire started.

I'd put the space heater in his room because our furnace had quit.

Melissa draped an Afghan blanket over the space heater.

You could say his death was on both of us.

15

The old guy was right—there was a sign.

Weathered gray and cracking like driftwood, the sign read in uneven hand-carved letters: Children of Fire. An almost-straight arrow pointed down a dirt road.

The road was barely big enough for my truck. Tree limbs and bushes *thwapped* and scraped along the sides.

I turned off the radio and with the windows open, I heard the sounds of birds and the rustle of trees swaying high above. Sunlight flickered across the path.

The way began to peter out and the underbrush crowded so close my truck was crushing a fresh path.

A felled tree blocked the way. It was too big to drive over and way too big to try to move by myself.

I wasn't even completely out of the truck before a woman appeared on the other side of the tree.

"Hi," I said. "I'm Landon Rowe."

"Welcome," the woman said. She was young, barely in

her twenties, long dirty blonde hair, and wearing a white tank top and baggy jean shorts. "You can leave the truck and follow me."

I closed and locked the door, my gun in the glove box and the tool bag on the passenger seat. I hated to go naked, but they were bound to search me. A weapon can be a wonderful persuader, but it shouldn't be a good detective's first option.

She gestured for me to follow her and started walking away. She was barefoot and stepping consciously but not cautiously.

"That's it? You don't want to ask me anything else? See ID?"

She glanced over her shoulder. "You're here. That's all I need to know."

"God brought me, huh?"

"Sounds good to me," she said.

I followed her deeper into the woods.

16

I typed Brock a text—*Arrived. Will keep u posted.*—but the blue sending line couldn't quite make it to the SENT finish line.

The woman didn't say anything else, and neither did I, until we came to another large tree blocking the path. Two people were sitting on the tree. They stood.

One was a middle-aged woman with long pigtails, the other a middle-aged man in a long-sleeved flannel jacket in which he must've been sweating like crazy.

"New arrival," the first woman said.

"I'm Rowe."

"You have to remove your shoes and socks," the woman with pigtails said. She was barefoot, her feet grimy and dark, and her jeans were equally dirty. Wedged along her hip under a wide leather belt was a very large hunting knife.

"I don't think so," I said.

The man in the flannel straightened and tried to puff his

chest. There was a bulge under his arm that might be a gun in a holster. He was tall but slender and held his hands before him as if in prayer. Dirt caked his fingernails.

"You have to," the pigtails woman said. "It's the only way."

I could've asked about Melissa and Eli, but nothing would stop them from lying. And what good would it do if I shoved my way through? Would the woman use that knife on me? Did the man have a weapon hidden on him somewhere?

The three of them were watching me.

I unlaced my boots and pulled off my socks.

"I'll take them," the man said.

"I could've left them in my truck."

The woman in the shorts shrugged as if she had no idea this was going to happen.

I handed them over. I'd had that pair for almost ten years, replaced the sole twice. The leather was incredibly soft and creased but strong as ever.

"I'll expect those back," I said.

The man did not respond.

After a moment, I asked, "What now, should I take my pants off, too?"

"Why are you here?" Pigtails asked.

"God brought me."

Her hand went to the knife, rested there. "God works in mysterious ways."

"Absolutely."

"*How* did you get here?"

I thought of saying I drove here, but I figured my sense of humor would be lost on this crowd. "Father Benny—Benjamin Reed—sent me."

Pigtails and Flannel Man exchanged glances and then gestured to the woman who'd led me here.

"Okay," the woman in shorts said. "I'm Pash."

"Pash?"

She smiled a pair of dimples. "That's Mo and Zebu." She pointed to the woman and man. They betrayed no emotion.

"Please tell me those are real names," I said.

"What else would they be?"

Total bullshit.

"Come on," Pash said. "It's not much farther. You're in time for afternoon meditation."

"Will everyone be there?"

"All the children of God," she said.

And of fire, I thought.

17

I'm not sure what I expected, perhaps a bunch of camping tents and some poorly constructed wooden altar (and a burning ceremonial fire, of course), but what Pash led me to was more like a summer camp.

The path gradually widened until the ground was nothing but well-beaten dirt, and then we came to a clearing. Three wooden cabins with open screened windows were lined up on one side of the clearing and an open pavilion was on the opposite side, picnic tables set up inside it. Two people were setting the tables. Lunch and meditation?

"Gee, didn't realize I was attending a retreat."

A large field of lush grass filled the space between.

But I did get one thing right: in the middle of this field was a big fire pit, encircled by large rocks. Firewood and kindling was stacked nearly six feet high. Ready for the next burning.

They light some big fires, I'll tell you that, the old guy at the gas station said.

"Where is everyone?"

But Pash wasn't listening. She stood several feet in front of me, head tilted back into the sunlight, arms out, palms open.

I heard a voice somewhere, perhaps coming from one of the cabins, but I couldn't make it out.

Was everyone hiding and secretly watching me from the bottoms of those screened windows or from around the trees at the far ends of this clearing? Assessing me as a threat? Readying their weapons?

If this were a horror movie, I'd probably say I got a really bad feeling right then and knew I'd made the wrong decision.

Being a cop and then a detective, however, changed my reaction to such situations. I was used to walking into horror-movie scenes. A dead guy in a puddle of his own vomit with a needle jutting from his arm. A bruised and bleeding woman sobbing on the front steps of her home as her husband glared at her from across the yard, all of us knowing she wasn't going to press charges. A severely dehydrated and emaciated child squinting against our flashlights as we pulled back the false wall and found where his deranged uncle had been keeping him.

I've seen some fucked-up shit, no question, so a summer camp in the middle of the day with a bunch of Jesus freaks didn't even quicken my pulse.

"Where's the head honcho?"

Pash lifted her arms until they were above her head and stretched her fingers. "Right there," she said and dropped her arms and turned like a game show model revealing a prize.

Eamon Fischer stood on the other side of the fire pit.

As if he'd been there the whole time and I simply hadn't seen him.

18

Older, yes, and skinnier, but otherwise Fischer might've stepped right out of that VHS video. His hair still straggled long but had grayed, a yellow bandanna keeping it off his face, and his jeans were so faded and worn thin they might be from the nineties. His shirt was plain blue.

"Welcome," he said. "I'm Eamon Fischer."

We shook hands. His smile looked genuine. But true sociopaths know how to manipulate others; most can easily beat lie-detector tests.

"Landon Rowe."

"What brings you to us, Landon?"

"Most people call me Rowe."

Fischer kept smiling.

"I'm looking for someone."

"Ah." He slipped an arm around my shoulders. He was tall and his arm reached easily. "We're all looking for someone... or something."

"I'm not speaking metaphorically," I said. "Melissa Rowe. Sorry, Melissa Jacobs. She's my ex-wife."

Fischer nodded as if I were confessing some injured part of my soul.

"I know she's here. Her son Eli is with her."

"I understand," Fischer said.

"Okay, where is she?"

He was looking right at me. His eyes were incredibly blue. Melissa probably loved that, right along with most of the women here and some of the men, too, for that matter.

"What is it you're after? She's not your wife anymore."

"Let's call it doing a favor," I said.

"I will. A favor."

"So, where is she?"

He released a long breath. "You see all this?" He gestured to the pavilion, the cabins, the fire pit. "It's humble. It's not much. But it is everything. Do you know what I mean?"

I shrugged off his arm. "I don't care what you have. I'm not on a crusade. I just need to find my ex-wife."

Again, he stared at me. He didn't blink. The day had warmed considerably and the sun was now beating down. I licked my lips and tried to swallow what little moisture I might have in my mouth. Back in the truck was a bottle of seltzer.

"God brought you here," he said.

"No. It wasn't God."

"All things serve God, whether they want to or not."

"The ultimate catchall, how convenient."

"I apologize for the formality," he said. "Mo and Zebu were no doubt curt with you. Pash is delightful but she can be distant." She had walked off toward the pavilion but stopped and was reaching for the sky again. "It creates the wrong impression of who we really are, but we must be cautious. Vigilant."

"In case the locals try to drive you out for being Satanists?"

He made a face I've made a million times when musing about the stupidity of my fellow man. Criminals who recorded their deeds on cellphone video. Perps who bragged of their crimes to friends. Idiots who got stoned and passed out in the getaway car.

If criminals weren't so stupid, a lieutenant said to me years ago, *being a cop would be a hell of a lot harder.*

It wasn't only dumb criminals; it's dumb people. People who believe police should be abolished. People who stormed the Capitol because they believe in some pedophile pizza cult or whatever the hell it is. People who believe Bill Gates put tracking devices in the COVID vaccine. People who believe every conspiracy theory and who question every fact. People too dumb and too irate to be held responsible for their behavior.

Infuriating but true.

I could imagine the local town board and the chief of

police stomping through the woods with a cadre of angry moms in tow, some with cardboard signs declaring there's only one Jesus and he's in a church not the woods, and maybe others carrying actual pitchforks. Few things are more dangerous than moms who think they're protecting their children.

"We're a peaceful group," Fischer said. "This isn't a cult. I'm not some zealot who makes the women be his wives or who abuses children."

This guy was affable, even charming, and though I knew it was an act, a persona, I couldn't help but like him back. At least a little.

"Yet you call yourselves Children of Fire."

"Children of God was already taken." He smiled. "They call themselves 'The Family' now, as if that makes up for their warped beliefs and terrible abuses in the name of God."

"I thought you said everything serves God," I said.

"It's warm out here, let's get you some water."

19

"How's the feet?"

We were at a bench at one end of the pavilion.

I took a long swig from a bottle of spring water he'd handed me and gave my feet a glance. They were already dirty and bleeding from a few pinpricks on the soles.

"They'll adjust quickly," he said. "Develop calluses."

"I won't be here that long. Besides, I like my boots."

"The Earth, the ground, is charged with God's power."

"And boots are the work of the Devil?"

At the other end of the pavilion, two men in shorts and t-shirts were setting places at the picnic benches. Instead of plates and flatware, they were putting a sheet of paper and a pencil at each spot, as if preparing for some self-help workshop.

Maybe that's exactly what it was.

"Nice place."

"Thank you. You're welcome to stay as long as you'd like. We have plenty of room, food, and water."

"How do you survive the winters?"

"We survive just fine. We winterize the cabins. We're meant to live in every season, and with God's help we flourish on even the coldest of nights."

"I saw a video of you," I said.

He searched his mind. "You mean at Minnewaska," he said. "That was a long time ago."

"Twenty years," I said. "How long before you move on to another place?"

He sighed and I gulped more water. Even in the pavilion's shade, I was warm and getting warmer. The day was thickening, too, getting sticky and heavy.

"I think we've found our rightful home, here," he said, except I heard a note of self-deception.

"Until they force you out."

"Doesn't matter. I've been many places. I've helped many, many people find peace. Doesn't matter where I go or who I meet. God is with me. I am His servant."

"So, what is it?"

"About God?"

I gestured a thumb over my back toward the pit. "Fire," I said.

"Ah, yes," he said and clapped his hands together, elbows on the table. "Modern ideas have corrupted our thinking. Fire is bad. Hell is the eternal fire. The Devil is made of fire."

"He's not?"

"When God first speaks to Moses, do you know how He does it?"

"Loudly?"

"Through a burning bush."

"Must've been quite the sight."

"It was a fire that burns eternally but does not destroy," he said. "If God so wills it."

"So, God's a pyro?"

"The Bible speaks of the 'unquenchable fire' of Hell, yes, but it also speaks of the 'fire of Heaven' as the 'glory of God.' The word of God, the voice of God, is described as fire itself. The Lord creates a pillar of fire so the exiled Jews can see in the desert at night. The Lord consumes burnt offerings through whirlwinds of fire that descend from Heaven. God burns away sin and pain and hate. He baptizes with fire. In the Gospel according to Luke—"

I held up my hand. "You don't have to ply your trade on me."

"Interesting way to put it."

"How would you put it?"

"Speaking the Lord's truth."

One of the guys putting out paper and pencils started setting them on our picnic table. He was mid-twenties, skinny, with a thin sag of beard. He looked exhausted. The paper was that super-cheap unlined grey stuff they used to give us in school and the pencils were the kind you get when you golf.

I drank more water but couldn't seem to wet the back of my throat.

"Thank you, Ephram," he said, and the guy nodded and moved on to the next bench. Was he cowed? Drugged? Indoctrinated?

Or maybe just tired.

"When do you turn into Tony Robbins and make people walk barefoot across burning coals?"

"That's a gimmick, not genuine faith."

"You burn crosses into people's chests."

He nodded and a slight smile played at the corners of his mouth. Did he find me amusing? Predictable?

"I don't subject anyone to that. It's a choice. Most people here haven't done it, but those who choose fire do it because it is a physical symbol of their spiritual devotion."

"Couldn't they just wear a cross?"

"I understand where you're coming from, I do. We're not a typical group of parishioners. This isn't a typical church. You know where the Kingdom of Heaven really is?" He touched the center of his chest. "Here. It's in your heart. You don't need to go to some stone cathedral. You don't need to put money in an offering plate every Sunday morning. You need only *believe* and be true. That's what faith is. And in return for that faith, God will give you everything you need to truly know happiness and love."

"That's quite a promise," I said.

"It's not mine. It's God's."

"Where's everyone else?" I made a show of looking around. Pash was still on the grass, sitting crosslegged now, face tilted up. Meditating perhaps. "What about the vaccine? Are you vaccinated against COVID, or does God keep you safe?"

"You don't trust us, do you?"

"I don't trust anyone who puts their faith in make-believe. But if it's any consolation, you don't strike me as a Satanist."

"You think it's make-believe?"

"A man in the clouds? An omnipotent being that sees all, knows all, created all? Yeah—make-believe."

He glanced around and, credit to him, summoned something near awe. "The world is such a magical, glorious place. You think it happened by accident?"

"I think it's pure arrogance to believe it didn't."

"And yet for thousands of years, people have spoken of and worshipped God."

"Well, of course people *want* to believe in a god," I said trying to sound like a musing professor but no doubt coming across like my arrogant, prick self. "People look at a leaf or at a sunset or at their own hand and can't imagine such things could be random. People don't want to think they are mere animals. There must be a purpose for why we're here. It's all got to add up to something, right? And as for God, well, He lets bad things happen because He's trying to teach a lesson or because we're still paying the price for original sin or because He has some grand, mysterious Plan with a capital P that we can't possibly fathom."

He considered me for what felt like a long time. Again, he didn't blink but he didn't seem to be straining, either. He was completely untroubled and that bothered me. Call it my *cop sense*, if you want.

Or maybe more of that good ol' paranoia.

"You have a lot of pain," he said. "You need to let it go."

"You think so, huh?"

"I'm sorry for what happened to your child. Ethan, was it?"

"Melissa told you."

"Here, we call her—"

"I don't care. The name thing is too cultish for me."

"Merely symbolic. It's easier to be true to yourself when you can step out of yourself."

"Is that what we call a paradox?"

"What is it you really want?" he asked.

"I told you—I need to see my ex-wife, Melissa."

"And yet you're engaging in this conversation."

I drank more water. "Where are the children?"

"They'll be here any moment."

He was smiling.

"You know why I'm really here," I said.

I heard the sounds of people approaching through the woods.

"And here they come."

"God can remove your pain," Fischer said. "He can burn it away."

"No branding for me, thanks."

"May I give you something, Landon?"

"I'll be straight with you, Eamon. I don't have my gun. You took my boots. But if you or anyone else here tries to stop me from what I'm here to do you're going to regret it."

He moved fast, quick as the strike of a snake, but not to hit me. He snatched my Field Notes memo book from my breast pocket. He picked up the golf pencil next to him, tapped it on the book the way some smokers tap their cigarettes before lighting, and opened to a random page and wrote something.

"Oh, I hope it's a bible quote," I said.

He handed the book to me and though I didn't want to give him the satisfaction, I couldn't resist flipping pages until I found his penciled scrawl.

God forgives you.

"Cute," I said.

It took me a few tries to slip the ledger back in my pocket.

He was watching me, unblinking.

I was about to say something, perhaps even tell him to fuck off, but the people from the woods finally emerged.

Women. And with them, the children.

PART FOUR

20

I'd counted almost a dozen women before I saw Melissa. Half of those women had a child with them, each one around the toddler age. Maybe one or two who were closer to double-digits. One of the women was heavily pregnant, one hand on her belly, the other holding that of a four or five-year-old walking beside her. Some women wore summer dresses, others jeans or shorts, and the kids were a mess of splashy colors and cartoon characters.

Summer camp, I thought. *Jesus Summer Camp. Come children, gather around the fire and let us speak of our sins and pain.*

My thoughts might be a bit too close to reality.

When Melissa and I were together, she favored yoga pants and colorful tops but now she was wearing green overalls and a long-sleeved shirt underneath. Her hair used to be long and dyed blonde but now it was her natural brown and shorn into a near buzzcut.

She held the hand of a small boy walking beside her. SpongeBob grinned off his shirt.

I started to get up and, quick as when he grabbed my memo book, Fischer snagged my forearm. "Stay," he said. "Sit. Join us."

"I'm not one of your disciples."

"No, you're one of God's."

I kept getting up, even called out to her, and he gripped harder. His fingers squeezed pulsing blood. He was surprisingly strong.

"When the state troopers came here and questioned her," he said, "it was very upsetting. She's made great progress but that interaction distressed her greatly. I cannot allow that to happen again."

"I'm going to talk with Melissa now," I said. "And you can take your hand off my arm."

But he didn't.

"You're going to sit down. You're going to join us for afternoon meditation. Do that, and I'll grant you audience with your ex-wife. Otherwise, I will remove you."

The thing about religious fanatics, or any sort of fanatic—antivaxxers or those QAnon nut jobs—is that they completely believe everything they say and there's no such thing as going too far to defend what they unquestionably know is true.

I could've handled Fischer, a sucker punch to the gut,

another to the jaw, or maybe a simple chop to his throat, but I still didn't know how many people were here and how many might be a real threat. There was also Mo and Zebu to think of, especially that large knife on Mo's belt and whatever might be under Zebu's flannel jacket.

I sat back down.

"Wonderful," Fischer said. "And her name is Nebu, not Melissa."

Fischer released his grip and stood, arms out in welcome. "Time to pray."

On cue, the doors of the cabins banged open and more people emerged.

Mel, or Nebu, stood with her child outside the mass of congregating people. The others were talking and their children were talking. They all seemed to ignore Melissa and her child, as if they knew she was nuts.

Fischer said she'd made "great progress" but the troopers questioning her "distressed her greatly." What did those two things mean? What did "progress" look like for my ex-wife? And how was she showing distress? She used to disappear for all-day hikes or go several days without showering or jump from a yoga retreat in the Catskills to a Buddhist retreat in Canada to a "Life Dream" retreat in Hawaii in a manic desperation and each time she'd float back on a cloud of revelation that darkened and turned stormy.

I'm on a soul quest.

We'd fight. She'd yell and blame me for everything, for ruining her life, for being so oppressive, and then she'd collapse on the bed and cry for a full goddamn week. She'd lock herself in the bathroom for hours and emerge swollen-eyed with hashmarks bleeding on her wrists.

I drank the rest of my water but my mouth felt cottony and my throat itched. Maybe I was allergic to something out here.

Mel was not looking at me, though she'd seen me before when I called out to her. She was staring at the ground like a scolded child. Her son, however, was staring at me.

He was a good-looking kid, but his eyes were wide and scared. Desperate.

Pleading for help.

21

I should've known.

In my defense, I'd been out of the detective business a while. What was I supposed to do? I was thirsty. He offered water.

My dry mouth.

My itchy throat.

Fuckers.

22

The important thing was to remain calm.

I'd done acid a few times back in my college days and when the floor liquified and tentacles slipped off the walls to snatch at my eyeballs with fleshy hooks, my roommate grabbed my face with both hands and told me to focus on my breathing. *It's just a trip, man,* he said. *You're taking a trip.* His skin rippled like a dead animal's infested with maggots.

There were no tentacles with hooks trying to snare my eyes, not yet anyway, but everything was blurring as if I were looking through a rainy window. My head felt both hollow and also too heavy to move. The bench was sticky and I made exaggerated movements trying to peel my arms off the wood.

A rat on a glue trap, I thought.

The tables filled with people. I tried counting but kept losing track. Easily two dozen. Maybe thirty or even forty.

Only adults.

Where have all the children gone? I sang like Peter, Paul, and Mary.

Someone sat across from me where Fischer had been.

I heard my voice trying to carry a tune and put a hand to my mouth as if I were a child who couldn't stop himself from speaking.

I couldn't see whoever was across from me. Worse than blurry, this person was a sunspot that made me squint and it hurt my head to look right at whoever it was.

"This isn't some religious event," I said. My voice sounded a little drunk and also felt like it was coming out of my ears instead of my mouth. At least I wasn't singing. "This is a cult. I've been drugged. I'm ending all this. Say bye-bye."

But I couldn't move. Maybe I was stuck. Maybe my legs weren't getting the command.

Just a trip, man. Taking a trip.

And going nowhere.

The person across from me said nothing.

"We praise the Lord," Fischer said. He stood at the opposite end of the tent, everyone else seated and facing him.

"Lord, hear our praise," the people responded.

"Let us pray," Fischer said.

Complete quiet—

Except I heard every inhale and exhale, every sniffle, every cough, every swallow, every creak of a bench as someone adjusted how they sat, every papery flap as a humid breeze passed through, I heard even the slip of a tongue across lips, the peel of a shirt from a sweaty chest, the crack of a knuckle, and crazy as it may sound, the liquid push of blood in the carotid arteries of whoever sat across from me.

We know the phrase "time dragged," but when you're drugged on some hallucinogenic, time no longer holds the same meaning and so the notion of it dragging doesn't make any sense. It's more accurate to say time *melts*, you know, like that Dali painting.

I heard birds in the distance.

"Amen," Fischer said and everyone said it back to him. The person opposite me sounded like a man, voice deep. *My bodyguard,* I thought. Except that wasn't quite right. He was here to guard the others *from* me.

I heard children whispering.

"Don't move," the man across from me said.

He was glowing as if made of light.

"You an angel?" I asked and laughed.

"We are here," Fischer said, "in this time and place because God wants us here." He opened his arms, surveyed his congregation. He was wearing a draping robe, purple and green. *Priestly vestments.* "They say we live in scary, uncertain times. Who can disagree? Our planet is on fire. Protests fill our streets. Violence. Crime. Injustice. The Sixth Extinction is upon us. COVID was a warning. The plague has only just begun. Something much worse is coming, and it's almost here."

"Is he always so sunshiny?" I asked and gurgled laughter.

"Shut up," the guy said.

"Wouldn't God want you to be nicer?" Was I really this much of a smartass? I could punch myself.

"Every generation," Fischer was saying, "believes it has it the worst. Wars. Famine. Destruction. Every generation believes the End Times have come. Perhaps we are always correct to believe that. Humanity's existence is a blink of God's eye. Time holds no meaning because God is eternal. He never began and He will never end. He simply *is*."

"Actually," I said to my guardian angel, "time is slippery when wet." That got me snorting laughs again.

"I told you to be quiet," he said.

"No, you told me to 'shut up.'"

Fischer kept going, saying something about New York. "We were ousted from our previous home, but much like the Jews who wandered the desert for forty years, we know what we have been promised—and we *will* get it. The glory of His love will keep us buoyed, and in the end, we will know His blessing."

"Where have all the blessings gone?" I was Peter, Paul, and Mary*ing* it again.

"Shut up."

"Each faith believes it is the chosen faith, the most righteous one." Fischer grinned. Even through the melting blur, I saw that smile. A charmer's smile. A con man's grin. "But we know where real faith resides, don't we?"

"Oh!" I shouted. "I know this one."

No one even glanced at me.

"The psalms say, 'O Lord, you have examined my heart and know everything about me.'"

"I knew it was the heart," I said to the guy across from me. "That's where the kingdom of heaven is. Funny that it fits in there, you know?"

"You cannot hide from the Lord," Fischer said. "He knows all. He knows your sins. But He wants you to acknowledge those sins. We must cleanse ourselves. We must come to God with open hearts and ready souls. 'Create in me a clean heart, O God, and renew a steadfast spirit within me.'"

"Maybe we can burn them out of us," I said and laughed.

Instead of telling me to shut up, my guard chuckled.

"Just you wait," he said.

"Faith unites us, yes, but it is not about faith *among* us. It is about faith between you and God. You do not confess your sins to us. You do not share them. Not even with me. You confess them to God. Make your sins tangible so you may purge your pain, your guilt, and your sorrow."

Fischer appreciated his congregants (*cultists*), nodded, and sat between two people at a bench up front. As he took up a golf pencil so too did everyone else.

People blurred into fleshy blobs that stretched and drooped like melting taffy. *The Persistence of Taffy*, I thought, imagining Dali's painting again. People wrote, and I heard the trace of graphite across the uneven indentations of the picnic table beneath each paper.

Even the guy across from me was writing.

I wanted to ask if his sin was a lack of a sense of humor.

But he was glowing again and I couldn't look at him without hurting my eyes. Other people were glowing too, as if electricity were suddenly illuminating them. In-between these sunbursts, the melting taffy pooled on the tables and dribbled to the ground.

The paper before me was not melting. It took a few tries, but I picked up the pencil, tweezering it between thumb and forefinger, and then I was writing. Some drug-induced nonsense, most likely, but the compulsion to put pencil to paper was too strong to resist.

I wrote—and couldn't see what I was writing. The paper kept washing clean like water across a plate.

I strained to focus even as my hand kept writing. I tried to mentally mirror the movements of my hand in a kind of skywriting of the mind but all I got was jagged lightning lines in a shimmering darkness.

It was the drugs, whatever was in my drink, *obviously*—and yet I wondered.

Did my hand have a mind of its own? Was my subconscious in control of my hand? What the hell was I writing?

Betraying me, I thought. *Damn you, hand! Why are you doing this?*

The pulpy thump of my fists against flesh. The snap of bone beneath.

My hand kept tracing the lines of letters I could not discern, but I was dropping backwards into memory.

The splash of blood up my arm and across my chin. The sounds of people yelling and the yelping moan of the guy beneath me as I hit him again and again and again.

The acrid stink of something burning.

Smoke. So much smoke.

I coughed and couldn't stop.

My lungs stuttered, chuffing air that seared along my throat.

Something was thudding my back in hard thwaps.

When I could breathe, Fischer was standing up front and sermonizing again.

"We are each a child of God, and therefore we must look upon our children as the purest among us. For Jesus said, 'Suffer little children, and forbid them not, to come unto me: for of such is the kingdom of heaven.'"

This earned scattered "Amens."

"Come, children," Fischer said.

They marched in from my left and lined up in front of Fischer. Eight or nine of them. Each time I tried counting, one of them would disappear or an additional one would be there.

I would've thought they'd each be in matching culty

uniforms, maybe black sweatsuits or goofy child-friendly shirts with grinning cartoon Jesuses on them or maybe a not-so-G-rated crucified savior with sallow face and bleeding wounds.

Instead, they looked like any group of kids in shirts and shorts (yet barefoot) who had just finished the playground circuit of swings and slides and monkey bars, their faces flush and exhilarated.

Or afraid.

One kid wore a Ninja Turtles shirt, another a faded Batman shirt with the shoulder seam splitting, another a dinosaur shirt.

Where was the SpongeBob kid?

Fischer spread his arms over their heads.

It's an auction, I thought. *Choose your child.*

And someone had already chosen Eli.

Shit.

"I knew it," I said, sounding drunk. "You're a bunch of pedophiles."

"Enough," my bodyguard said directly above me, slapping a hand on my shoulder to push me back down. I tilted my head and his glow slipped behind his wide shoulders and heavy arms.

Not a bodyguard or an angel. He was a bouncer.

I held up my hands in a don't-hit-me gesture. "Hey, man, I'm drugged. I don't know what I'm saying. But you can be straight with me. Which one of those kids is your favorite? You know, which one *really* gets you off?"

He punched me so hard I might've thought it the hand of God, except I didn't think anything.

I didn't even feel myself hit the ground.

23

There's always smoke even when there isn't fire.

You wake choking on it. Can't breathe, lungs burning, hands clawing at your throat as if you could stretch open the airway, and you dive violently out of bed into the pool of night, knocking over the lamp on the nightstand, bulb popping, and you smack the floor hard enough to knock in some air. Deep sucks. Too lightheaded to stand. But you do. You *must*.

Here's what you have to do: stay upright, keep moving, down the hall to the room that's been empty thirteen months, punch open the door, smack the wall switch and when the light won't come, convince yourself it's because the bulb burned out, not because the room is filled with smoke, convince yourself it's silent in here because it's empty, not because something that was breathing in here is now dead.

Here's what you can't fathom because it's the worst thing possible, the thing you can't know, a fear maybe, a horror you can try to imagine, but it won't be real, only those who know the reality could ever know any of it, and yet it means absolutely nothing.

How could it?

What meaning is there in a dead child?

I hear the crackling of fire. I feel its heat.

"Ethan!" I scream.

And I shoulder through the door—

Hands seize my shoulders. "Landon," a voice says. It's Fischer. The smoke is too thick to see his face and the fire is so loud he must be inches from me. "Release your pain. God wants you to let go. I will help you."

I have to get through all this smoke. Have to get to the crib. My child. My son.

"God forgives you," Fischer says.

"Fuck God."

Someone else is pawing at me, trying to wrangle me into a hug. "Landon, it's me," Melissa says into my ear. "Our boy is dead. Our dear little baby is dead."

"Bitch!" I scream and shove her off me.

There are others around. Gathered and watching. But they are shadows without faces. Fire licks into the black sky.

Hours have passed, it must be late now, and the fire pit is a raging bonfire. *They light some big fires,* the old man at the gas station said. People are whispering things, prayers, maybe. Or satanic incantations.

"God will cleanse your soul," Fischer is saying.

Melissa is crying against me in big sloppy sobs the way a child cries. "Our baby. Our baby. Our baby."

People crowd around me. Someone shoves me and then hands seize my arms and legs, pin me to the ground.

Fischer stands over me. Firelight plays on his face. The quivering shadows elongate his eyes into his forehead and hook his mouth into a jack-o-lantern grin.

The hands gripping me are strong as shackles. I feel the hard ground beneath me. I feel the fire somewhere to my left.

Do your worst, I try to say but what comes out is a slurred mess.

Fischer bends low. His face flickers in and out of shadow.

He's undoing the buttons of my work shirt. My undershirt is sweat-stuck to my chest. He flaps the ends of the shirt apart and leans within kissing distance.

"Release your pain. Release your sins."

I try to tell him to fuck off but my mouth can't form the right shape to make the words.

"I'll help you," Fischer says.

He reaches for something and then he's holding an iron rod over me. The end of it is a small cross, the size of my palm—and it's molten-fire red and sizzling. Smoke curls off of it.

Another set of hands yanks the collar of my undershirt halfway down my chest.

Melissa?

"Keep him still," Fischer says. He stands over me, glaring down, eyes huge, and the burning cross blazing in the night. "God will baptize you with the Holy Spirit and with *fire*."

He stamps that cross onto my chest.

I scream.

My flesh is searing, blistering, smoldering.

"No, no, no," I'm saying, voice frantic, panic rising up from deep within where the most horrible fears live, the ones we never articulate because vocalizing them might make them come true.

My arms stretch and stretch down through the smoke...

And pick up my child.

His face is ashen, his mouth scooped wide, his lips blue, his eyes open and lifeless.

"Ethan!" I scream.

The hallway is miles long until I crash into the kitchen counter and here next to the coffee maker and the toaster I perform CPR on my infant son.

Even as I'm pressing his chest with two fingers and then torpedoing air down his throat, I see the tiny white coffin engulfed in funeral flowers, I hear Melissa's sobs break into screams.

We bury our son in the cemetery on a drizzly August afternoon, my suit smelling of smoke, and I see both the coffin disappearing into the ground and the empty crib waiting back at home, the charred walls of the nursery, and I see the future where we remove the furniture, tear up the carpet, and scrub the walls and repaint, creating a guest room or a sitting room with a framed picture of Ethan on the wall, that one of him in his blue onesie where it looks like he's thinking mischievous thoughts—and I see into the past where I will forever be too slow to smell the smoke, too slow to run down the hall, too slow to grab my son, too slow to save his life.

You want there to be meaning. You want there to be more than a dead child and the acrid whiff of the smoke that killed him.

You want so much.

We hadn't had sex in forever, so we got drunk. That usually led to something. This time, it did, and we must've passed out, but I remember Melissa getting out of bed to check on Ethan. She walked into the hallway where the nightlight tinted her naked body green.

Then I was waking up coughing sometime later. Melissa was still asleep, curled away from me.

I thought I was having one of those dreams that seem so real you think you're awake, but then my lungs hitched and I hacked up coughs and got out of bed.

Smoke rolls in along the ceiling.

Still, I'm thinking it's a nightmare.

You don't know what a nightmare is... yet.

Life is cruel and that cruelty comes in irony so thick you want there to be a god you can chastise for creating moments so barbaric.

You run down the hall to your child who died while you slept, and for the rest of your life this moment will replay ceaselessly just below the surface of your conscious thought and every night you will wake with smoke in your lungs and you'll think, *There's still time*, but there isn't because this is only a nightmare. You can't change the past. But you can suffer it over and over again.

I taste smoke in the back of my throat. I must be in bed on the brink of enduring this horror yet again—*quick, get up, your boy's still alive*—and though I know it's only a nightmare, my boy is already dead, I also know he's going to keep dying again and again because there's no end to the smoke-filled hallway with that green nightlight, the CPR performed between the coffee maker and the toaster, the coffin lowering into a small hole as I rub at the skim of soot on my face that's been scrubbed clean and as Melissa collapses to the grass in a dead faint.

You expect your wife to stay on the couch day and night with the TV flickering across her. You expect her to grieve for weeks, months. To barely eat. Or bathe. Perhaps she'll try to drink herself to death or swallow a bottle's worth of Xanax.

What you don't expect is her to get up early and jog, to

be fresh-faced and smiley. You tell yourself she's still in shock and refusing to accept what happened.

Days go by and she's Mrs. Homemaker, the house scrubbed and vacuumed, the kitchen table a spread of pancakes and bacon in the morning with fresh-baked cookies in the afternoon and Betty Crocker dinners at night.

You try to talk to her about it but her smile cuts toward her ears.

Unhinged, you think. *She's going to snap.*

You imagine discovering the bathroom door locked with the fan droning on inside and you shoulder-pop the lock and find her in the tub, one arm dangling off the edge, blood still dripping off her fingertips.

Instead, she talks about Father Benjamin Reed, a priest you didn't even know until he officiated your son's funeral and burial.

He's been so helpful.

Our boy is in Heaven.

God has a plan, and we must have faith that He knows what is best.

You grunt in response and scrape knife and fork across the dinner plate.

She'd been flighty before, but since your son's death she's attending all the self-improvement seminars she can, each one in some hotel conference room, and she's disappearing for days at find-yourself retreats that are always in the woods or by a lake.

One day she says that's it, she's done; in fact, she's been cheating on you and even got knocked up—marriage over.

It's over for you, too; you just don't know it yet.

You'd been following a lead on a string of petty robberies, mid-day house break-ins, theft of jewelry, watches, loose change, and you had enough information to put together a sort of sting-operation.

But then you get thinking about Father Benny.

You go there. Block the driveway, red-and-blues spinning, and you grill him but he won't give you anything, not even after you punch him a few times.

Cops watch from the street.

Someone might have intervened if you'd kept going, but *Hey, his son just died and this priest talked his wife into leaving him so a few punches will be good for both of them.*

Any man would agree.

Even after Father Benny makes a formal complaint, no one really cares.

Until you catch the house robbers in the act.

They are a couple of strung-out twenty-somethings who'd been stealing whatever they could to hock at various pawn shops to get money to score smack.

You tackle a skinny guy in black jeans. Necklaces, bracelets, and rings erupt out of his hands. You flip him over. He's blinking nonstop, completely confused, fear-whited face.

You hit him. And hit him. And hit him.

That's how you get put on leave.

You need to relax, Rowe.

Then you walk out of the police station, get the 9mm you keep in your glove compartment and fire it at the chief's cruiser.

That's how you get fired.

This is bullshit, you say.

The chief nods, says something about not letting your feelings cloud your judgment, that you need to focus on getting better and coming back, but you're never coming back. *This is bullshit. My son is dead and I'm being punished for it.*

That's true. You weren't the one who left the Afghan blanket draped over the space heater.

You didn't cause the fire.

But you're the one condemned to wake with smoke in your lungs and the hall stretching all the way to a hole in the ground.

24

"Will you save me?"

Someone was standing over me. I tried to blink away the blurriness but everything was so dark I couldn't see anyway. My head throbbed and my eyes felt sore as if I'd been staring at a computer screen for days.

Or at a burning fire.

"Mister? Are you dead?"

Stars speckled the black sky far above.

"Who...?" My throat scratched into a cough that tasted like smoke.

God will baptize you with the Holy Spirit and with fire.

Flesh-Searing fire.

I sat up, muscles cramping and spasming through my back and across my shoulders. I didn't hesitate, didn't flinch, just went for it—pawing at my shirt and pulling down my undershirt, the scream of pain tunneling up my throat, and slapping my hand to my chest.

Where the skin was smooth and unburned.

I hallucinated the whole thing.

It took me a moment to catch my breath.

I expected to be in the grass field near the fire pit, but I didn't even see the cabins or the pavilion. I was in another clearing, the trees surrounding fifty yards back, but I had no idea where I was. I didn't see any fire. I could be miles away.

They dumped me here.

"Mister?"

It was a child. I couldn't make out his face.

But I recognized the shirt and the grinning cartoon character on it.

"Holy shit," I said. "Eli."

Another hallucination.

But I snagged his wrist, grabbing too hard and yanking, and he collapsed onto me.

He clutched at me with his little hands.

"They're going to kill me," he said. He was crying, chest hitching. "Help me!"

For a moment, I couldn't respond, but then I hugged him back, feeling his solidity. He smelled as if he hadn't bathed in quite a while.

I felt something in my chest that made me think of lava flowing through charred capillaries of scorched earth.

"I got you," I said. "You're okay."

And I was okay, which bothered me for some reason.

Fischer drugged me and all that followed was a hallucinogenic dream.

They'd tried to scare me, that's all.

Come back and we'll really burn you.

Had someone actually said that?

I straightened the kid into a soldier at attention, asked if he was hurt. He shook his head.

"How did you get here?" I asked.

Tears rolled freely down his face. They glowed like tiny pearls. "They're all asleep," he said. "I left."

Sneaked away. Good for him.

If criminals weren't so stupid, being a cop would be a hell of a lot harder.

Maybe the same could go for cult members.

Grab the kid and go, I told myself.

"Why? Why did you run?"

He wiped the back of one hand across his snotting nose. "There's a burning. They're going to hurt me."

Would they really brand a cross onto a child?

He stopped crying, stared at me. "They're going to kill me."

"No," I said. "They're not." I stood. "Let's get the hell out of here."

I lifted the boy and hugged him against me.

We fled into the woods.

PART FIVE

25

When I was nine years old, my favorite movie was *Die Hard*. It was one of the few VHS tapes we had, the cover showing a high-rise tower with the roof exploding, and I watched that movie every damn day for months and months. My parents never voiced concern.

I could quote the movie by heart, and did all the time, but mostly I ran around the house pretending to be John McClane trapped in Nakatomi Plaza, shooting bad guys with my toy handgun, and growling out his one-liners. I'd run into the living room, aim at the lamp, and make shooting sounds and then say, "Welcome to the party, pal."

My *Die Hard* infatuation finally got the attention of my parents when I went too far recreating the iconic barefoot-and-broken-glass scene. I had to get the real effect, so I took a wine glass out of the cabinet, did my best impression of Hans Gruber saying "Shoot the glass," and hurled it onto the wood floor. Shards exploded everywhere.

Unlike John McClane, I was not able to make it across the room to safety. With my very first step, a curled fang of glass punctured the soft middle of my foot and I screamed and cried until my mother came in the room and saw me writhing on the floor and Bruce Willis on the TV.

All of that came back to me within thirty seconds of running. I was barefoot, of course, and now forty pounds heavier with Ethan hugged on my hip. John McClane never had to do this. And at least he had a gun.

I was managing to step on every twig and rock. Something sharp as a razor blade sliced my left foot and something else equally sharp cut the right foot, perhaps next to my *Die Hard* scar.

I could now see at least ten feet or so in any direction, but I had no idea which way to go.

I'd never taken a survivalist course, had not been a Boy Scout, and my military training, though good, was not SpecialOps. Yet I knew you could use a stick to make a sundial—if there was sunlight—to then orient yourself without a compass. I also knew I could follow the North Star to get my bearings. I only had to find the Big Dipper.

But the problem still remained: I didn't know which direction I was supposed to go.

Where was my truck?

A branch slapped against my face and I stopped. Every direction looked exactly the same.

"Where's camp?" The kid didn't respond. "Which way'd you come from?"

He was crying again.

Shit.

"It's okay, Eli." I gave him a squeeze, patted his back. "We can do this."

Sometimes new cops or cops newly promoted to detective would ask if I had any advice. *Trust your gut and always look like you know what you're doing,* I would say. *And if you fuck up, take responsibility.*

I adjusted my hold, and we continued on.

26

I heard something.

Off to our right, maybe fifty yards, maybe less—something tromping through the woods, branches snapping, heading our way.

I froze.

The kid kept his grip on my shirt with one hand and plopped the thumb of his other hand into his mouth.

Another branch snapped with a firecracker pop.

Coyote. Bobcat. Bear.

Then: voices.

"This way," a male said and other voices, maybe three, maybe more, responded.

Flashlight beams crisscrossed through the trees.

Headed our way.

I turned and got moving again, but with the very next step, my right foot took an impaling that had to be a rock but might as well been that shard of wine glass I stepped on years ago.

The lights swooped through the dark and caught me even before I could bite down on my shout.

You catch a deer in headlights and it can't move. Its eyes dilate, its vision is completely useless, and it freezes. It's no different for a human staring into a direct spotlight with eyes that had adjusted to the late-night dark.

Except, I had a hand that could block the light.

"Don't move," someone said.

"Every time I said that to a suspect, you know what they did? They ran."

Four flashlight beams slid across my face and body—and across Eli.

"Happy trails," I said and started to turn.

"Landon," another voice said. It was Fischer. He crushed twigs and leaves directly in front of me, cutting the distance rapidly but without a sense of urgency. Just fluid movement. The flashlight beams caught the edge of his silhouette. "How are you feeling?"

"Feeling?" I asked.

"I drugged you."

"No shit."

"Sometimes it's necessary in order to—"

"Stop," I said. He did, both in word and deed. "I'm leaving and taking Ethan with me. We can do this the easy way or the hard way. Point me in the right direction and I'll go. Try to stop me, and this'll turn ugly."

"Of course," Fischer said.

"Just like that?"

"We don't want violence."

"Only drugs and fire?"

Fischer took another step. He was within fifteen feet. The flashlight beams knotted at my throat.

"You can leave," Fischer said, "but the child must stay."

"Well, then," I said, "looks like we have a problem."

Somewhere close an owl hooted. A mosquito buzzed in my ear. The kid shifted against me.

"You don't have any idea what you're doing," Fischer said. "But I understand. You're in pain. I can help you. *God* can help you."

"Baptize me with fire?"

"You don't even realize what you're saying."

"I don't, huh?"

"You just called that boy Ethan."

My dead son's name coming from Fischer's mouth made my eyes burn.

But he was right. I had said Ethan.

"Point the way," I said, "or I will make it my mission to destroy you and everything you've created."

"I haven't created anything," Fischer said. *"Everything* is God's work. He may give and take as He sees fit."

"How wonderful."

"You aren't responsible. You didn't kill your son."

"No shit," I said. "My wife did."

"No," Fischer said, speaking calmly, coming closer. "We are each an instrument of His will."

"Stop moving," I said.

"That boy is not your son."

"Shut up."

"You want to save him, I understand. But he's not in danger. *You* are."

"One more step, and I will fucking kill you."

He stopped, didn't move. The others stopped as well. The flashlight beams stayed anchored to my neck.

The owl hooted again.

"Don't let them hurt me," the boy said around his thumb.

I tried to swallow the acrid skim of smoke in my throat.

Movement to my immediate right, something pushing through the brush.

Another of Fischer's followers, and once he was on me the others would move in. I couldn't fend them all off and protect the kid. I had to run.

"A few hundred yards to your left," Fischer said, "you'll find your truck."

Whatever was moving toward me stopped. A raccoon, perhaps.

"It better not have flat tires or a missing battery."

"Of course not. Your keys are still in your pocket. We're not the enemy. We're doing God's will. I want to help you, Landon. I really do."

My body flushed heat. I hadn't thought to check for my keys, but I felt them in my pocket pressed against my thigh. My phone wedged in the opposite pocket, I tugged it out and used the flashlight function. Why hadn't I thought of that sooner?

"Do not follow me."

"You'll be back," Fischer said.

"Don't count on it."

"It is God's will."

27

They didn't follow, at least not so closely I could tell.

With the cellphone flashlight shoving back the darkness, I cut through the woods quickly. Every step hurt—my feet were bleeding, skin hot and wet—but I didn't slow down.

Gee, I said to myself, *if you'd been smart enough to remember you had your damn phone you would've been in your truck by now.*

Although that wasn't necessarily true (without Fischer telling me, I wouldn't have known what direction to go, assuming he told me the truth and I wasn't heading right back to his camp and some fiery ritual), I could not stop the gerbil wheel of self-critique spinning in my head.

I'd gotten rusty these past many months.

You mean watching Netflix endlessly and passing out on your couch with empty beers scattered around doesn't keep you mentally sharp?

And hasn't it been closer to years than months?

I stopped, glanced around. It all looked the same.

What if Fischer hadn't pointed the way to my truck or to his camp but simply off to endless nowhere? We'll wander until sunup.

"We're lost," the kid said.

No, shit, I thought but didn't say.

Trust your gut and always look like you know what you're doing. And if you fuck up, take responsibility.

"We're going to be okay," I said.

So much for responsibility.

But then I heard it—a sound so common in everyday life and yet so wonderful to hear in this moment.

A car passing, tires on asphalt, engine revving.

There was another part to that advice I'd give new cops and detectives: *When in doubt, hope you get lucky.*

Luck is the best kind of police work.

It's also the best kind of salvation.

I hurried toward the sound.

28

I almost crashed right into the side of my truck. Wouldn't have mattered to the truck, just one more dent among many, but I stopped in time, cellphone flashlight blinding a reflection hard as a punch.

The kid was safely in the passenger seat, my tool bag dropped in the footwell, and I was telling him to let go of me everything was okay we're getting out of here—when someone stepped in front of the truck.

Starlight silvered the outline of a tall guy, not hefty but draped in something that could give the impression of girth. A flannel jacket.

He had something in his hand.

"You can't leave with him," Flannel Man said. What was his name, Zeke, Zed, Zorro?

"Okay," I said loudly inside the truck's cab while jawing down the glove compartment. "I'm coming out."

Now, the question was whether that bulge I'd noticed under his flannel earlier was a gun in a holster.

"Slow!" Z-Man said. "Nice and easy, back out of the truck."

Maybe the guy *had* been a cop but more likely he'd simply watched too much TV.

I moved fast, stepping back from the truck, bringing up my gun, aiming just to his right.

"One move and I'll put a bullet in your gut," I said.

My gun was a Beretta 92FS, same as John McClane's.

"I'll do it," I said. "Trust me."

He pondered that.

I shut the passenger door and walked around the front of the truck. Z flinched but my gun stayed on him and that kept him in place.

"You have no right to do this," he said.

I unlocked the driver's door. "Sure I do. It's God's will."

What happened next happened really fast. I've been involved in violent interactions (ones that were not my doing) and when it happens you simply react (or don't). Adrenaline floods your veins and you do what you have to (or not) and you make it out (or you don't). What's funny is you may not remember exactly how it happened. One person's experience can be completely different than someone else's. Perception is everything. The guys in Internal Affairs make whole careers out of that. They definitely had fun with me a few times.

Best I recall, it happened like this: I pulled on my door

handle, the door sometimes sticks and did this time, and Z-man flicked on the flashlight he was holding and hit me right in the face as he called out *"Now!"* and someone rushed at me from behind. I turned and Flannel Man's partner Pigtails was right there coming at me fast. Even when things happen in the time it takes to blink, you pick up on details. The crazed look in her eyes, the crease of her forehead, the gleam of light riding the sharp edge of the knife in her hand. I knocked her knife-wielding arm aside and swung the butt of my gun directly into her head. It cracked her in the temple and she was knocked out before her body bounced off the truck. Z-man screamed and charged.

I shot him.

29

Twenty minutes later, we're on the highway headed east and my phone spasmed with successive messages.

I ignored it because I was trying to think where my bullet had hit Flannel Man. He came running at me, perhaps yanking a gun from its holster or maybe armed only with a flashlight, and I fired at that beam of light. I might've even hit it because it spun out into the darkness like some whirling firework, and I waited but the night gave only the buzz of mosquitos and the distant hoot of that owl.

You shot that guy and left him to die.

You murdered him and fled.

Yeah, well, I doubted Eamon Fischer would go running to the police.

Besides, I was rescuing a child from a cult that, for all I knew, was planning to burn that child to death in some psychotic sacrificial ceremony.

Is that really what you think?

Yes, yes it was. The kid basically said that.

They're going to kill me, he said.

Does that sound too farfetched? I was no expert in cults but I knew about the poison Kool-Aid at Jonestown, and those Nike-wearing, comet-hopping Heaven's Gate idiots, and a Google search would bring up all sorts of sex cults and self-abuse cults and child-molestation cults and who the hell knew what else.

And you know what connects all those people? Belief in superstitious nonsense.

What's the difference between congregants in a church on Sunday and Fischer's people in the woods? Perhaps not all that much.

Or maybe you're trying to rationalize away your responsibility for killing someone.

In the passenger seat, the kid was sucking on his thumb, his legs pulled up to his chest, bare feet nearly tucked beneath him.

I took out my phone. A mess of texts and voicemails. I called Brock.

"What the hell is going on?"

"Relax," I said and regretted it immediately.

"*Relax?* I'm not going to relax. You said this would be quick. What the hell happened? What is going on? Did you find Melissa? Did you—"

"*Hey!*" I shouted and the kid flinched back against the door, making me feel like shit. "I have him. *I have Eli.*"

"What? You got him?"

"Yes."

"Is he okay?"

"He's fine."

"Where are you?"

"Heading back. Get in your car right now, head west on 17. I'll call you when I find a rest stop."

"Okay, okay," he said rapidly.

"One more thing," I said. "What shoe size are you?"

PART SIX

30

I drove another forty minutes before parking beneath the yellowy wash of light at a rest stop where a concrete edifice looked more like something from a horror movie than a public bathroom. Maybe that difference is negligible.

I called Brock, told him where I was, and hung up just as he was asking to speak to his son.

"Your dad will be here soon," I said.

There was one other car in the lot, a sedan parked at the far end, and two tractor trailers along the edge by the trees.

"You want a snack? A juice or something?"

The kid didn't respond. Didn't even move his head, but his eyes were shoved all the way in my direction. Scared of me.

Maybe he should be.

I used a grease-stained old dishtowel from my tool bag to go at the blood and dirt on my feet, but I stopped after a few useless smears.

You go into law enforcement because you want to help people. You want to have the badge and the gun to sort out the good guys and the bad guys. You want to rescue the weak and innocent and punish the cruel and corrupt.

You want to do the right thing.

Like shoot an unarmed man who was only running at you because you bashed his girlfriend in the head with your gun?

She was trying to stab me, let's not forget.

You showed her. Imagine what it was like when she woke up and found Flannel Man on the ground in a puddle of blood. Maybe he was still alive, barely, face pale and blood bubbling between his lips.

I'm not a murderer.

Who're you trying to convince?

"You're safe," I said. "Your dad's on the way. Everything is okay, I promise. You don't have to be scared of me. I'm a detective. I help people."

You mean, were *a detective.*

Vending machines should be stocked with beer.

I scanned through the texts and listened to the voicemails. All were from Brock save two. Brock's texts and voice messages each got slightly more frantic and angry until he was begging for me to respond in one breath and threatening to have me arrested in the next.

The only voicemail not from Brock was from my supervisor at the security company where I worked. They hire out mostly retired cops to work as security guards. I was supposed to be guarding some office building no one gave a shit about enough to rob.

The only text not from Brock was from Melissa. She must've stolen someone's phone to send it.

Her text was simple: It's Melissa. Stay away.

Was she looking out for me?

Maybe she doesn't want you murdering more of her cult friends.

You know why most people drink or do drugs? To silence the voices in their head. I don't know if it's true, or even could be proven true, but I think cops have more voices in their heads, or at least more vocal ones, than the average idiot.

Or maybe I just want to tell myself that because I'm no good at silencing those voices.

People who hear voices are usually insane, though, right? Either that, or it's good old-fashioned guilt. That's right, Landon, I'm your favorite voice, never-ceasing, ever-vigilant, always accusatory—your guilty subconscious.

Arguing with a voice that's in your own head never accomplishes anything, which is where the beer comes in. Drown the voice in booze and even if it doesn't shut up, it gets cocooned in a beer blanket that muffles its prattle.

It's almost 3 AM and you're stuck at a highway rest stop with your ex-wife's 4-year old child, so it looks like you're shit out of luck.

And with that, the rollercoaster of memory slowly *clank clank clanks* up the steep incline into the sky and there's no getting out, not from way up here, only thing you can do is try to brace yourself as you crest the top and hold on as you plummet and your stomach scoops your heart into your throat.

The ride starts with the *bang* of my gun firing and the *thunk* of it cracking skull or breastplate and then we're off in a backwards memory trip through Landon Rowe's greatest hits. Firing a few bullet holes into the chief's cruiser. Tackling that house robber and beating his face into ground beef. Punching Father Benny a few good ones in the gut. But the coaster flings hard to the right and left and there I am interrogating suspected drug dealers and prostitutes with the assumption of their guilt and the power I wield to intimidate and threaten while pretending to be "good cop," and now we're rocketing upside down in one loop after another as I reach across interrogation tables to yank confessions from people's throats, and there's one more steep stomach-hollowing plummet as I make a wife-abusing asshole swallow fragments of his own teeth broken beneath my fists and his bruised wife screams for me to stop and I threaten to knock some sense into her next.

Wow, with all that taken into consideration, it's not much of a surprise you shot Flannel Man. Face it, Landon, you murdered that guy, and the only surprise is that you at least never killed anyone as a cop.

But I was trying to do good.

No, you wanted to hurt the world the way it hurt you. But you can't get back at Death for killing Ethan. When it comes to death, you can't do anything except be its victim.

No point disagreeing.

The truth is the truth.

31

A car sped up the in-ramp so fast it might've been a drunk driver, or someone about to shit themselves, the headlights bobbing, bottom of the car carving sparks in the speed bumps. We were coming out of the bathroom, the kid had to pee and it took him a while, he standing at a urinal while I was at the door where a dying fluorescent light flickered moth shadows across a wall of obscene graffiti, both of us barefoot and bound to get all sorts of bacterial and fungal infections, and then we headed out into the path of a car speeding right at us.

Brock didn't park in any of these open spaces but instead screeched to a stop at the curb where I was holding the kid's hand so he wouldn't run out and get himself killed. He didn't turn off the car, either, just hopped out and ran around toward us.

"Surprised you didn't get pulled over," I said.

"Eli, Eli," he was saying over and over.

Brock hesitated a moment, something like uncertainty on his face, and then he hoisted the kid in a feet-off-the-ground hug. Brock's red sweatshirt enveloped the kid.

"Mission accomplished," I said.

No reason to tell him about the guy I shot and maybe murdered.

Brock looked at his son, tears on Brock's cheeks, and slowly, he got to his knees and was face-to-face with the boy.

"What the fuck, Rowe?" Brock said.

"What?"

Brock stared up at me. "This isn't Eli," he said. "This *isn't* my son."

32

There were vending machines inside, though none with beer, and for a few bucks the kid got a bag of Cheetos and Brock and I got shitty coffee.

We sat at one of the concrete picnic benches on the grass. The night was cooling off, the humidity releasing its grip, but the chill settling inside me needed more than a coffee to warm it away.

"He was with Melissa," I said. "Holding her hand. What the hell was I supposed to think?"

The kid, whoever he was, ate his Cheetos slowly, one after another, head down.

Brock fumbled with his phone, stabbing and swiping and cursing. *"This,"* he said finally, "this is my son. *This is Eli.*"

On the phone, a small boy grinned around a melting ice cream cone, vanilla covered in rainbow sprinkles. Ice cream dripped off his cheeks. The boy was clearly Brock's son—you could see the same facial structure just beneath the child-soft skin, like looking at a sculptor's in-progress work. Same eyes and ear-shape, too. But what struck me was not the face because I couldn't recall the faces of the other children lined up in front of Fischer. What I could recall was the faded Batman t-shirt on one of those kids, the same shirt this ice cream-eater wore. The insignia nearly washed to nothing, the shoulder seams splitting in a small mouth.

I chose SpongeBob when I should've chosen Batman.

"He was there," I said. "I saw him."

Brock's hands became fists, knuckles red, a scab on one of them hanging loose, and then he opened them and massaged them together. Trying to keep himself under control. "Bitch," he said, shaking his head. "She knew. Christ, she knew how to fool you. Wasn't difficult, I guess."

"You think she knew what she was doing?"

"Yes. She did this on purpose. Tricked you. Made you think..." He gestured to the kid who stopped eating but wouldn't look at us.

"You're sure—"

"What? That this isn't my kid? *Fuck, Rowe.*"

"Calm down," I said, saying the exact wrong thing.

"Calm down? You were supposed to get my son, not some random child."

Fists again, he hammered one hand on the table, lucky not to shatter all the bones in it. The kid flinched, dropped the Cheetos.

"Look," I said, "we'll go back. We'll get him. Together."

I was trying to think how that could work but he wasn't listening.

"I should've known," he said, shaking his head. "Those people are nuts. Troopers couldn't do anything. *You* couldn't do anything."

He kept talking but they were under-breath mumbles.

"Let's go. We'll go right now."

That cut through. "I can't."

"We're getting your son."

"I can't go back."

"Get in my car—. Wait, what did you say?"

He didn't respond.

"Hold on," I said. "What aren't you telling me?"

He was off in a self-ramble again.

"Brock—"

I snatched his fist and squeezed. He was a bigger man and his hands were heavier, but my fingers were just as long as his and my grip just as strong.

"What did you not tell me?"

He wanted to hit me. I saw that clearly, and I thought of the Estwing hammer in my truck.

A car passed on the highway.

"I was there," he said. His fist let go and so did I. "I went there with her and with our son."

I wasn't sure which question to ask first.

I wanted to smack him. Or hit him with that hammer. Maybe I should. Guys with rage issues usually understand violence.

"You were there and didn't think it important to tell me?"

"You didn't ask."

"Don't get cute. Why didn't you tell me?"

"Christ, Rowe. It's embarrassing."

"Embarrassing? This isn't about you. It's about your son!"

"I know! Don't you think I know that?"

"I don't know what you know, apparently."

"It's not like I'm withholding some vital information."

"I'll decide what's vital. Tell me."

"This was months ago, back in March. You know how she is, gets it in her head, and off she goes. So, I stop her, say I'm going with her. I thought she might cancel the whole thing, hoped she would, but she was giddy for the idea.

"So, we went up there, as a family. The people are okay, I guess, but they're all misguided, you know. The no-shoes-or-socks thing is stupid enough, but they're living in the woods with this grey-haired hippie who branded his chest with a cross. It's nuts. But they walk around with dumb smiles on their faces like it's Kumbaya summer camp.

"Wasn't my scene, sure, but then the asshole drugged me."

"Fischer?"

"Yeah."

"Me too," I said. "It was in the water."

"Might as well be Kool-Aid," Brock said. "I had all these hallucinations. Thought they were going to set me on fire. I woke up in the middle of the woods and when I managed to find my way back, they wouldn't let me in. Said I'd hit somebody."

Better than shooting somebody, I thought.

"I refused to leave without my son, and eventually Fischer brought him to me. He made me wait, standing there with his hands on my son's shoulders. Said my boy was a 'child of fire' and his place was there with them. I told Fischer to take his fucking hands off my son or I'd set *him* on fire."

Brock chuckled. "He did. Pushed my son toward me, and I took Eli and left. That's the thing about people like Fischer, cult leaders or whatever they are—they're really just cowards."

"You didn't think you needed to tell me any of this?"

"What difference would it have made? She came back and everything seemed okay. She was at home with our son. Life went on. I thought we were good. Then this. Had I told you, what would be different right now?"

I opened my mouth and closed it again.

"Please," Brock said, grabbing my wrist. "Bring me my son."

I stared at him. I was pissed and wanted to yell at him for not telling me everything, but I also understood. He didn't know what he was doing. He married a woman he thought he could control and she ran off with their kid. He was wracked with guilt and shame and rage. He wanted a little help, that's all.

"Okay," I said.

The kid dared to eat a Cheeto. I'd called him Eli and he hadn't corrected me, but I'd also called him Ethan. Christ, the two names had become interchangeable in my head. "What's your name?" I asked.

The kid hesitated. "Eli?"

"No," I said. "Your *real* name. And not whatever bizzarro one Fischer gave you. Your *real damn* name."

"Please," he said and finally looked at us. "Don't make me go back."

"Why not?"

He swallowed. "They're going to kill me."

"Why do you say that?"

Another swallow.

"There's a burning," he said. "They're going to hurt me." Verbatim what he'd said when he found me in that field.

"I'm going with you," Brock said. "We're rescuing my son."

"No, you're not. You can't. You just told me that. *I'll* take care of it. You take the kid back to your place. Or to mine, I don't care."

"You're going to drive back now and get him?" he asked, frantic.

"Are you sure he's even there?" I asked.

"Where else would he be? I've checked with Melissa's mom and the few friends she has. No one knows anything."

I was nodding and thinking through how I could get the kid. A smash-and-grab kidnapping would be tough, especially since I didn't know where in the camp Eli, the *real* Eli, was.

"Rowe?"

"Go home. Watch the kid. I'll be in touch."

I got up, started for my truck and stopped.

"You remember to bring me shoes?"

"No," Brock said. "Must've slipped my mind."

33

I didn't even turn the truck's engine before I got back out. Brock hadn't moved from the bench and neither had the kid.

"Change of plans," I said.

34

Before leaving the rest stop, I texted Melissa.
Brock is coming for his son.
Ten minutes later she texted back.
Stop him or Eamon will kill Eli.

I was driving when I read that. Good thing no one else was on the road.

PART SEVEN

35

The sun was creeping over the mountains when I took the exit for Tabes. The sky streaked purply bruises. Fischer might say such natural beauty was proof God had created this world. Even if that were true, it was a poor consolation for a world that also killed children.

I stopped at the same gas station. Filled up with the same gas, and walked inside to find the same old over-tanned man working the register.

"You're back," he said and leaned his elbows on the counter like we were old friends about to continue a previous conversation. He noticed my bare feet and waited.

"Got a question for you," I said. "Two actually."

36

Ironically, it was harder to find the Tabes Fire House than it'd been to spot the wooden Children of Fire sign. It took driving the wrong way down a one-way road. My head was still screwed up from whatever Fischer gave me, but a large cup of coffee and a butcher paper-wrapped cruller from that gas station started clearing the mental clouds and anchoring my stomach.

One of the firehouse bay doors was open and I walked right in. A lone fire truck gleamed a fresh clean. Somewhere a radio was playing classic rock.

"Help you?"

A young guy in a blue Dickies coverall stepped out of a small office on the other side of the garage bay.

"I'm looking for the Fire Chief," I said.

"Who're you?"

"Landon Rowe. I was a detective downstate."

"*Was* a detective?"

From behind him appeared a guy around my age, perhaps a bit older, certainly more grey and a little heftier. He had a thick mustache.

"You must be Graham, the Fire Chief?"

He nodded. "Need help?"

"I'd like to help *you*."

"How's that?"

"What do you think of those Children of Fire idiots?"

He rubbed his mustache, studying me. "Looks like you need some boots."

37

I called Brock.

"We're all set," I said.

"Okay. What's that mean?"

"Don't worry about it. You know what to do."

I was back in my truck and watching a kid pedal lazy figure-8s down the middle of the empty street. His shadow stretched and warped.

"Yeah," he said, "but I don't know what *you're* going to do."

"You don't have to."

I hung up.

Across the street standing in the open bay doorway, the Fire Chief gave me a slight wave. I returned it and started my truck.

No rest for the wicked.

38

I was never in the shit, as the saying goes, not even sent overseas, and so I enjoyed my time as one of Uncle Sam's enlisted because it was pretty much just hanging out, BSing around, and doing PT. Occasionally, we'd be sent out on what we called Neverland Missions. We'd gear up and head out into the swampy woods of Georgia or into the rocky forests of West Virginia or, in one lucky stint, onto the beaches of Hawaii. Most times we'd screw around, but once during one of those West Virginia make-believe missions, we were uncharacteristically serious. There were eight of us lurking through the forest. We were completely quiet, stealth. At one point, a trio of deer watched us pass. We were tense, on high alert, as if we really expected to find some secret Taliban hideout in one of the caves. I can still feel the bead of sweat slipping between my shoulder blades. Then someone, I think it was foul-mouthed Petey but it might've been Roark, oinked in perfect imitation of a pig. Then somebody quoted

Deliverance and we started cracking up so hard we had to stop right where we were and get ourselves together, except we couldn't. Every time we seemed under control, someone would snort an oink or make a fart sound and we'd be on the ground laughing so hard we were crying.

Good thing we were never sent to war.

That Oink Mission, as we came to call it, was all I kept thinking as I trekked through the woods back toward Eamon and his fire children. We'd been so serious, so deadly serious in fact we might've killed a hiker had we come across one, and then we were on the ground laughing and crying and oinking.

Crazy how fine of a line there is between one thing and another.

At least Graham had given me boots. They were a size too big and well-used to the point of fraying at the seams and peeling around the sole, but any sort of protection was better than going barefoot. I'm not one for maxims but you can take my word for it in this case. When in doubt, boots are better than no boots.

This path cut through the woods from a cross street. It was longer than the other way where the hand-carved sign arrowed which way to go, but that wasn't an option. I shoved through tall skinny trees and tangled messes of thorny shrubs and snaggles of underbrush that would've mauled my bare feet beyond comprehension—so yeah, thank God for boots.

It would take a dump truck knocking trees and smushing everything beneath its tires to clear a useable path.

Which is almost exactly what Graham had in mind.

He and his crew had already cleared a decent path, except from where that path stopped to wherever the hell the camp was might as well be uncharted wilderness.

Instead of a machete or a dump truck, I had my Estwing hammer and my gun, but neither would do much to help slash through this mess of bushes and branches.

The gun was tucked in the small of my back and the hammer was wedged inside my belt along my hip, much the way the woman who attacked me had kept her hunting knife. *You mean the woman you smashed in the skull.* My hands weren't free, though. I carried two five-gallon red plastic gas cans, what some guys on those Neverland Missions called jerrycans. I'd bought them at the gas station, along with the gas sloshing inside them.

Gun, hammer, gas cans.

Meaning, you look insane.

No, I look prepared.

Sure, to kill somebody. Or many somebodies. One down, dozens more to go. In for a penny...

"I'm not going to kill anyone," I said through my teeth.

Stop him or Eamon will kill Eli.

Was Melissa's text genuine or was it more subterfuge because she wasn't yet done with this particular soul quest?

Regardless, my objective was simple: find Eli and hustle him to freedom.

Except it won't be that simple because the last time you were here you knocked one person unconscious and shot another, or have you forgotten?

I should've grabbed a six-pack, even a case. I didn't need to get drunk, just buzzed enough to smother those voices.

Drink all you want, nothing cliche about a former detective who's drinking himself into an alcoholic stupor because it sure beats owning up to what he did. Nope, nothing cliche about that at all.

I did what I had to.

You murdered that man.

Self-defense.

Is that what we're calling shoot-first, self-defense? Maybe you should call it preemptive self-defense. That at least sounds litigious.

With the next step, I tripped over a root looping out of the ground and stumbled several feet, catching a tree trunk and barely avoiding a direct face smash.

I cursed aloud before any mental voice could chastise me.

That's okay, I'll wait until you're done to then remind you that you're heading back toward the place where you murdered an innocent man. Talk about cliche, you're the killer returning to the scene of the crime. And what's with the hammer and gun thing? Are you some sort of domestic Rambo or something? Oh, no—you're John McClane, right? Yippee ki yay.

A scream burned in my chest. I get how people can be going about their day seeming completely normal and *BAM!* they just lose it, attack coworkers, assault a stranger, fire bullets into a crowd.

Anything to show that internal voice who's boss.

You realize you sound crazy, right?

Not even nine in the morning yet and the day was hot and getting hotter, humidity thickening the air into invisible Jell-O. I was sweating, my head hurt, and I wondered what the hell I was doing.

You're trying to save the day, be the big hero, by being a total idiot. What was it you believed about being a detective, that it gave your life purpose? You think saving your ex-wife's kid will make up for all the really awful shit you've done? That somehow doing that will balance the scales?

Shut up.

Sure, of course, I'll do whatever you want. I'm just a voice inside your head, you can shut me up anytime you want… except you don't want me to shut up because you know I'm right. You murdered a man in cold blood.

Shut up.

Okay, let's talk about who else you hurt? You think of anyone? Maybe someone small and helpless?

Don't you dare.

You didn't check on your infant son and that's why he's dead.

Here's another piece of advice: don't talk back to your inner voice. You can put that right up there with the boots-are-better-than-bare-feet truism.

Think of him, your son, poor little Ethan, not yet able to walk or even crawl, never mind speak, can pretty much cry and wet himself he's so helpless, and you never bothered to get out of bed and walk down the hall to give one final check because you told yourself Melissa had just done it, but you knew better, you had suspicion, you'd seen it over the past several weeks, the languid slump of her walk and the purpling crescents under her eyes, and that time you found her motionless before the open fridge, the light glowing around her, and you snapped your fingers in front of her face not once, not twice, not even three times, but four times to get her attention, so you knew you should've checked on Ethan, on your son, your only child, but you didn't and that Afghan blanket smoldered and caught fire and the smoke filled the room where all Ethan could do was breathe it in until it started to hurt and then he cried for you but you didn't hear because a half-dozen beers makes for good earmuffs and you slept while your boy—

I screamed.

It barreled out of me and through the woods with ferocity enough to scatter a flock of birds into little black shadows against the morning's pale blue sky. If I were a painter, it'd make a damn good picture.

Last time I painted anything, I was in elementary school

and got more paint on my father's shirt, worn backwards as a smock, than I did on the paper in front of me. The art teacher said I was her little Jackson Pollock, as if I knew who that was.

Ethan will never get to wear your shirt as he slaps and splashes paint in a class full of children laughing and happy, full of life.

Another scream was coming.

I oinked instead.

A single piggy nose snort was all it took.

I chuckled, just for a moment, no rolling around on the ground bursting tears and trying to breathe through the pain of laughter, just a single chuckle and balance was restored.

Enough to keep moving, anyway.

39

Five minutes later, I found the camp.

One of the cabins was directly in front of me. I ducked in case someone was looking out the screened windows, but I didn't hear anything. I creeped close enough to peer around the side. The field, the fire pit (fresh wood stacked like a teepee and ready for burning), the pavilion—no people anywhere.

Brock as decoy may have worked too well.

Be honest with yourself: it wasn't Brock as decoy, it was the kid as bait.

I stopped again at the edge of the cabin, listened.

Rustling movement and voices but not from inside the cabin. Somewhere across the field.

There was a path over there, the one Melissa and the other women had been coming back from with the parade of children. I'd been talking with Fischer. Yeah, and he'd been drugging me.

I worked fast, backtracking aways before heading across the field.

I'd barely finished and was just past the fire pit when the same parade from yesterday was coming back from the same path in the woods.

Melissa, in the same overalls as yesterday, was behind the heavily pregnant woman, her belly practically in need of a sling. And next to Melissa was a small boy—in a faded Batman shirt.

More women and children were behind her. They all moved slowly, faces drawn, like they were on some death march.

Or in the midst of a ritual, I thought.

There's a burning, the boy had said. *They're going to hurt me.*

And you saved him. Good job. Oh, wait, you left that poor kid, who'd only wanted to escape these crazy people, with Brock who was headed right back here as bait. That's some damn fine police work.

"Melissa!" I called to her.

The pregnant woman stopped, both hands gripping her belly. A young girl peered from behind her legs.

Melissa almost walked right into her. The Batman kid pointed at me. The others stopped and stared, some of the kids asking who I was.

She didn't say anything until I was within fifteen feet.

"Here, my name is Nebu."

"I give a shit."

"You shouldn't be here, Landon."

"And I don't want to be. I'll leave right now. Give me Eth—*Eli.*"

She pulled her child closer to her. The boy stared, dumbfaced. I could take out my phone and look at the picture Brock had shared but the shirt was the same, no question, faded printing, shoulder seam splitting.

Melissa stepped out of the procession line, tugging her boy beside her, and said something to the others I couldn't hear. All those eyes staring at me, women and children.

Guilty, those eyes said. *We find you guilty.*

"It's okay," Melissa said. "Go on."

Gradually, the pregnant woman continued on her way and the others followed, progressing across the field toward the cabin I'd just been hiding behind.

One of the women, mid-thirties, straw-like hair stiff around her ears, leaned close to Melissa and whispered in her ear. Melissa nodded, and gave the woman her son's hand. The boy took it eagerly, a smile spreading wide on his face, but it disappeared as he watched me in a sidelong stare, heading off with the woman.

I could grab him and run, but that wasn't how I wanted to play this.

I hadn't lugged those gas cans for nothing.

"It's shameful Brock sent you," Melissa said. "He knew you wouldn't be able to separate your child from his."

Sunlight sparked off one of the buckles of her coveralls. She ran a hand through the buzz of her hair.

"You're forgetting, Melissa, that both kids are *your* children."

I longed for anger to tighten her face but it didn't happen.

"You don't care? You've run off to this place with these fire-loving freaks and you could give a shit what your real sins are." I hooked my sleeve up onto my shoulder. Our son's baby feet tattooed there in ink as black as what they used at the hospital to print them after he was born. "Remember what you said to me when I got this? You said it was in bad taste. Our son was dead and you said this"—I stabbed at the tattoo—"*this* was in bad taste."

"I'm sorry," she said. "I'm so terribly sorry."

"Fuck your sorries."

"Landon, you can find peace here. Believe me. I have."

I chuckled. "Peace? You look like shit."

She stepped toward me.

"Fire killed our son," Melissa said. "But the fire of God will save him and us."

I could've smacked her.

"Fire didn't kill Ethan. *You* did."

She flinched. "I know you hate me. I accept that. But I want you to stop hating yourself."

I shook my head, forced another laugh. "Fuck this. I'm taking Eli and leaving."

She grabbed my arm, and I glared back at her over my shoulder.

"That boy isn't Eli," she said. "He's just wearing his shirt."

"Bullshit."

"I knew Brock would show that picture of Eli. The ice cream, right? He loves that one."

"What the hell are you saying?"

"The police were easy. A pair of troopers questioned me and I said I didn't have a son. Said he was dead. They assumed I'd gone nuts, probably, just another crazy cult person. They barely looked around. I thought he might go to you. Shameful, like I said, but predictable."

"And you're trying to trick me right now."

"No, Landon, I'm not. I've caused you enough pain. Did Brock tell you he came here with me and was forced out?"

"He was drugged, just the way I was."

"Brock was abusing me, Landon. He hit me all the time. Slaps mostly, but punches too. Never in the face, though. He was smart about it. Bruise up my back. He broke a rib once. I took it, accepted it. I thought I deserved it. Every time he hit me, I told myself it was my punishment for what happened to Ethan."

My eyes were burning and I hated her intensely in that moment. How dare she try to make me feel bad for her.

"He came here with me and Eli. But Fischer saw him slap me and kicked him out. He wouldn't leave, of course, so Fischer drugged him."

"But Fischer handed over his son, *your* son. Why would he do that if he knew Brock was an abuser?"

She swallowed. "Fischer believes all things serve God's will. He believed my son would be returned to me. And he was."

"You've gone completely insane. You know that, right?"

"No," she said. "I've never been more sane than I am now, Landon. I went back to Brock so I could save my son. That's what matters. That's what God wants me to do."

"You want me to believe that kid in the Batman shirt isn't your son? Then where is he?"

"I'll show you," she said and tugged my arm.

I didn't move.

Thought I heard something.

Deer maybe, or birds.

"Show me what?"

She gripped my arm harder. "My son."

40

I followed her into the woods from where she'd come. The path was well trod, about two-people wide, and the trees gave way to a field of high grass and wildflowers.

"I know what you think," Melissa was saying, "that we're all crazy. Anyone who does something like this *must* be crazy. How could anyone be in a cult, right? And, yes, I can say the word because that's what it is—a cult. But you know what? The first Christians were a cult. Jesus' Disciples were the original cult."

"Yeah, yeah," I said. "I think I heard this already."

She stretched out both arms so her palms touched the tops of the wildflowers. "We're not idiots."

"I don't care. That's not why I'm here, Mel."

She made a musing sound. "You haven't called me that in forever."

"Sorry, I forgot your cult name."

"He has a name for you, too."

"Do tell."

"Ira."

"That's disappointing."

"In Latin, it means 'the wrathful one.'"

She'd slowed her pace, tilted her head into the sunlight.

"Tell me," I said, "how often do you fuck Fischer?"

"You don't understand."

"Sure, I do. It's standard cult leader agenda—isolate the women, give them bizarro names, and fuck them."

She stopped, turned to face me.

"You're hurting," she said. "You're in so much pain."

I thought she might touch my face, perhaps even kiss me, and the possibility of such tenderness pissed me off.

"I *am* hurting, and you should be hurting too. You should be hurting *a lot* more."

"I'm sorry," she said.

"Save it."

"This isn't who you are." Her hand did come up then but retreated. "You're a gentle man, a kind man. You were such a good father—"

"Shut up."

"The Landon I know wouldn't have attacked two innocent people."

"They were trying to hurt me."

My internal voice did not object.

"You could've killed them."

I felt the weight of the gun pressed against my back, the hammer along my waist.

I wanted to ask what happened to them but she wasn't offering the information and I felt ashamed to inquire. Birds chirped. Bees did their thing from flower to flower, and a red-and-black butterfly landed on a branch and slowly worked its wings as if in quiet contemplation.

Jesus, what the hell was wrong with me?

"Where are we going?"

"I'm trying to get through to you, Landon."

"Don't you mean Ira?"

"Be serious. Be vulnerable."

I glanced around. "What's back here?"

"I'll show you."

My hand on her upper arm almost pulled her into me.

Many traits make a good detective. Observant. Inquisitive. Patient. Methodical. I had those traits, at least some of the time, but my best trait, the one I relied on every time when I was unsure, and the one that finally kicked in right then, was my gut instinct. There's no quantifying it, no explaining it—but it's *the* most important trait that can make a good detective.

Instinct.

"You're wasting time," I said. "Stalling."

Her face stone-hardened and she yanked from my grip. "Do whatever the hell you want. You always do anyway."

She kept going.

I followed.

Her bare feet kicked up little clouds of dirt. Her skin must be as hardened as sneaker soles.

A little farther on and the narrow path opened into a small clearing.

It looked like another fire pit, a rock circle with wood set in the middle, but it wasn't a pile of wood—it was a cross set upon a two-foot-high base. Large stones were set around it and wildflowers curled every which way.

"What's this?"

"What do you think it is?"

"A burial site," I said.

It's where they buried the guy you shot, that internal voice said. *These religious freak psychos probably mummified him in sheets and asked God to raise him from the dead like Jesus did for that one guy, whatever his name was.*

Except I didn't believe that. Fischer was crazy but not *that* crazy.

"He's there," she said. "My child. My boy. *My Eli.*"

Her son, her second son, was now as dead as her first and buried here in the middle of the woods in Bumblefuck, New York?

"How'd he die?"

She was shaking her head, hand at her mouth. "I'm cursed. Two boys. Both dead. Why would God do this to me?"

She dropped to her knees before the gravesite.

We were at the cemetery, Ethan's tiny coffin lowering into the ground beneath Father Benny's unblinking gaze, and Melissa cries out, sounding like a loon wailing across a lake, and she puddles to the ground where I leave her as I bear witness to my son's burial.

My gut interrupted again.

This wasn't right. This wasn't real grief. She was playing me.

"Stop it," I said.

She was straining to cry and couldn't do it.

"Stop bullshitting me. There's nothing here. You're delaying until Fischer and the others get back."

Words played at her lips but nothing came out. It was an old tic of hers. It meant she wasn't telling me something.

I shook my head. "I'm going back and taking that kid, *your* kid, and getting him the hell away from this place."

"You don't believe me about Brock?"

"He ever hit Eli?"

Again, her lips moved without words.

"You ever think maybe he hit you because you deserved it? You ever think maybe you deserve to be hit every day of your life for what you did?"

I wanted her to spring to her feet and attack, hit me, spit in my face, scream, do *something*.

Instead, she released a long breath and her whole body deflated.

"Fine. Stay here."

She finally spoke before I was too far to hear, making me turn back.

"What?" I asked.

"You're right," she said. "My son's not dead. There's no body here. We pray here, that's all."

"Great. Thanks for wasting my time. Word of warning: You should stay right here. It'll be safer for you."

"Landon, wait."

"What?"

"That boy, in the Batman T-shirt, he isn't my son. He isn't Eli."

"Bullshit. I'm taking him."

"That's not him. Please don't."

"Nice try, Mel, but..."

Intuition spoke up again: but the boy had taken that other woman's hand eagerly, gratefully, a big smile on his face... because she was his *actual* mother.

"Then where is he?"

That words-at-her-lips thing again, but she didn't have to say. I knew. Not gut instinct this time, just snapping puzzle pieces together.

Mel was afraid for her son and knew hiding him here would not work because Brock would follow her here, or send the police, or even recruit me. I didn't know what the kid looked like, and Mel knew what picture of him Brock would show me.

The kid wasn't here. He wasn't stashed with his grandmother or at some friend's house. There was only place in Mel's warped thinking where her son would be completely safe—in the holy hands of one of Fischer's followers.

"He's at Father Benny's."

Not a stone face, no moving lips—simple, unadorned defeat. "I was afraid Brock would come here, so I left him with Father Reed. He'll keep him safe."

"Locked up in his prayer basement?"

"He's fine."

"You think so?"

"Why do you even care, Landon? Go back to whatever drunk life you have."

I went right for her. I'm not sure what I was going to do, but the compulsion was too strong to resist. Except when I got to her, she sat up, rising toward me, pushing from her knees, face like a moon gleaming between clouds, inviting my hand, even the hammer, begging for me to smack her back down.

"Do it," she said.

I could. I *really* could.

But I didn't.

I turned back around and left her there.

She called after me but I was quickly far enough away to pretend I was hearing things, the wail of some bird crying across a lake, perhaps.

PART EIGHT

41

I was reaching the pavilion when I heard the others approaching.

Unlike when Melissa and the other women and children appeared in somber death-march style, Fischer led this group as if it were Easter procession, his arms raised in praise and he was even leading them in some song about Jesus Christ the Empowered.

Might be a dozen or more. I recognized some of them from when Fischer drugged me, a mess of people with ripe body odor and dirt-smeared clothes. They were average people, typical everyday Americans dressed like they were getting ready to clean out the basement or garage, and yet somehow they'd come together here in the middle of Nowhere, New York, because they believed whatever shit Fischer was shilling.

I did not see Pigtails or Flannel Man. Of course not—one might still be unconscious and the other might be dead.

A big man, his blue shirt stretched across his heavy chest, walked beside Brock. *My angel bouncer,* I thought. I was surprised they hadn't tied up Brock. Hell, I wouldn't've been surprised if they'd carried him back hanging upside down from a log as if he were a fresh kill on a spit to be set over the fire. The kid, whoever he was, kept pace several feet to Brock's right. He looked terrified, like he might make a run for it, his SpongeBob shirt smeared like it was dragged through the dirt.

Brock, on the other hand, just looked pissed.

Brock was abusing me. He hit me all the time.

There were a couple ways to play the next move, but I didn't waste time weighing options. I drew my gun from the small of my back, raised it overhead, and fired a single shot.

I thought they might scatter like frightened deer, but instead they froze. The singing ceased. Fischer turned toward me slowly, his arms still raised in heavenly celebration.

"Landon," he said, sounding perfectly calm and unsurprised. "I knew you'd come back."

"I'm that predictable, huh?" I lowered the gun to my side.

"It is God's will."

Nodding, I walked toward him, cutting the distance to thirty feet or so, the fire pit between us. "Is it also God's will if I kill you?"

I aimed the gun at him.

Behind him, a woman in a willowy dress and a man in

a green polo took several unsubtle steps away from Fischer. Everyone else then had to as well.

"Some followers," I said.

"They don't follow me. They follow God. You do what you will, Landon."

"Nice. I love the martyr thing. It's very Christian."

He lowered his arms and walked toward me. A breeze twirled his long hair. People backed up farther. On the breeze, they could smell what I'd done.

"You're not going to shoot me," Fischer said.

"Why not?" Maybe he could see my finger wasn't on the trigger.

"You almost killed Matthew. He's at the hospital. Wendy is there with him. She has a bad concussion but she's at Matthew's bedside praying over him. You should go there, visit with them. Seek forgiveness."

My mouth stretched around words I didn't want to say.

"They forgive you. I forgive you. God will forgive you, but you have to seek it, have to ask for it, have to want it."

"Well, I guess that's the problem," I said. "I don't play make-believe."

"Do it!" Brock yelled. "Shoot the fucker!"

Wide eyes and scared faces peered through the screened windows in the cabin.

"Matthew and Wendy, huh? Don't you mean Mo and Zebu?"

"Landon—"

"I thought I was Ira, the wrathful one. I like that. Sounds cool."

"Names are man's construct. God allowed Adam to name all the things of the Earth."

"Didn't God name Adam?"

"Is it a biblical discussion you want, Landon?"

"Enough of this shit," Brock said. He shoved his way out of the line and stabbed a finger toward Fischer. "Where's my son?"

"He belongs to God," Fischer said. "As we all do, for we are all children of God."

"Where is he?" Brock moved closer, his whole body rigid, hands curled into fists.

"He's not here, Brock," I said.

"Give me that hammer," Brock said. He held out a hand, fingers splayed so hard his palm blotched red and white.

"I said he's not here. But I know where he is."

Like a tide pulling back to reveal a hidden thing in the sand, Fischer's expression changed—recognition? worry? surprise?—and was hidden again beneath the smooth calm wash of his Holy Man persona.

Brock finally turned to me. "Then why are we still here?"

The others were baby stepping farther away. The kid was staring at Fischer.

Just before he said it, I knew who the kid was.

"Come here, son," Fischer said. "God has brought you back to me."

The kid shook his head.

Fischer got on his knees, spread his arms. "'As a father has compassion on his children, so the Lord has compassion on those who fear him.' Come to me, my son. The Lord has brought you back to me, as I knew He would."

The boy did not move.

"He's scared of you," I said. "Rightfully so from what he told me."

"There's no reason to be scared, son."

The kid's eyes darted from Fischer to me to the woods and back to Fischer.

Someone was coming up behind the kid, moving on slow, barefooted steps. She was wearing a plain tan baseball cap, but the blonde hair, tank top and baggy jean shorts were the same as when she greeted me at the fallen tree. What was her name, Pish, Posh, Pash?

At the same time, Brock was coming forward but stopped halfway between me and Fischer as if he couldn't decide where he really wanted to go.

"What's your son's name?" I asked. "He didn't tell me."

"His name is Isaac," Fischer said.

"That his real name or his bullshit cult name?"

"Isaac was Abraham's son, and God commanded that Abraham sacrifice his son on a burning pyre."

"So, bullshit culty name, got it. Isaac, you're coming with me. Come here."

The boy's eyes flitted. He was too scared to make a decision.

Pash was only five or six feet behind him but she stopped, a cat assessing its prey, readying to pounce.

"You can see why he's afraid," I said. "He thinks you're going to sacrifice him."

"We're not crazy people, not Satanists. We don't hurt anyone."

"You think the child would lie?"

"The Bible says the truth comes from the mouth of babes," Fischer said, "but we know the truth: kids have wild imaginations and when they hear something they can't comprehend it can easily run away from them."

"What about Isaac, the one in the Bible, what happened to him? Was it all in his imagination?"

Fischer grinned. Dressed differently, he might have been an aging game show host, his a Chuck Woolery grin, cheeks bunching beneath his eyes. "God sends an angel to stop Abraham just as he is about to kill his son, for now he knows that Abraham will do anything for God. It is a testament to the power of faith."

"You think so? Sounds to me like Abraham was out of his fucking mind."

Fischer again invited the kid to come toward him, and again the kid did not move.

If the kid moved, Pash would grab him.

"What are we doing, Rowe?" Brock asked.

"I'm surprised," Fischer said, still on his knees, arms still out toward his son. "I thought you'd appreciate Abraham's story a bit more. Considering what happened to your son, I thought you'd appreciate Abraham's plight."

"What happened to my son wasn't my fault."

"And yet God took from you your only child, your son, your"—*Don't you dare say it, you asshole*—"Ethan."

My finger slipped back on the trigger. "Everyone out!" I yelled. "Come out! Everyone in the cabins. Out now or he dies! Outside *NOW!*"

They'd been watching, knew I had a gun, so they came out. Maybe they followed God instead of man, but they didn't want to be responsible for Fischer taking a bullet in the skull.

It was mostly women and children except for a skinny guy who might not even be twenty. He flinched from the scene and hid behind the others.

"Please," one of the women said. A stained apron was tied tight around her. "We're all mothers and these are our children."

"Good, good," I said, loud enough for everyone to hear. "It's like the old Puritan days—get the whole town out to bear witness as we burn up the witches."

I sounded a bit crazed. Maybe more than a bit.

"Please don't do this," Fischer said. "Some of the people here are very hurt, very *hurting* people, but we are all committed to finding God's peace. We believe in God and peace and love. You can find that peace and love, too."

He thinks I mean to execute them, I thought.

Can you blame him? my old reliable internal voice chimed in.

Pash was creeping close.

"Brock, grab the kid."

He started to turn and stopped, staring right at me. Only no, he was staring past me.

Brock was abusing me, Landon.

There she was, Melissa, coming back as if everything were completely normal. She'd cried out her tears, prayed to God, and now here she was, an overall buckle undone and swinging as she walked.

Brock made a heavy grunting sound and headed toward me. Toward her.

He hit me all the time. Slaps mostly, but punches too. Never in the face, though. He was smart about it. Bruise up my back. He broke a rib once. I took it, accepted it. I thought I deserved it.

I kept my gun on Fischer but gave Brock a stop sign with my other hand.

He kept coming.

"Let him," Melissa said behind me.

Every time he hit me, I told myself it was my punishment for what happened to Ethan.

"Brock, stop!"

That got him hurrying, rushing right at me, a linebacker going for the sack. His anger had gone from moderate and steady to apoplectic and completely unrestrained.

"You bitch!" He snarled the words, loud and phlegmy. "You took my son! What did you do with him? *Where is my son?"*

I wasn't going to shoot him, so I grabbed the hammer from my belt but before I could even get a good grip to swing it, Brock punched me in the jaw. My head snapped to the side and my jaw felt like it'd snapped out of its socket.

The hammer slipped from my hand but it didn't fall with me as I thumped to the ground. It went with Brock. He raised it high over his head, silhouetted against the blue morning sky.

"Where is my son? *Where is he, you bitch?!"*

I have no idea how close he was, couldn't tell from my angle on the ground, or if he was bluffing or really meant to hit her, but he was snarling curses in loud jumbled sucks of air, and that hammer was high in the air and ready to swing, so I shot him.

42

A textbook shot between the shoulder blades and just to the right of his spine. He stumbled several steps, Melissa screaming a shout and falling out of the way, and away from the arcing hammer.

Brock took a face-plant to the ground and I swear I heard his nose break and the ground vibrated beneath me. He was still, but certainly not dead.

People started screaming then. Not everyone, but enough of them, and that got them moving. They pushed one another. People fell. Children cried out. I expected Fischer to tell everyone to remain calm but he wasn't saying anything.

My gun was still in my hand. I put the safety on and went digging into my pocket.

On the ground as I was, the stink of gasoline burned strong enough to make my eyes water.

People were running around, some back inside the cabins, others thunking past in darting sprints.

And the fun was just getting started.

I checked the other pocket. Found it.

Someone was coming up on me.

"I don't blame you," Fischer said. In his arms he held the boy, his son, the kid's arms wrapped around Fischer's neck, but the kid was staring at me. His expression was pure fear. "You've been through so much. I don't know your pain specifically, but I know pain. I know only that those who have experienced pain can be especially cruel at inflicting it."

The fire pit was a good ten feet away. I wasn't injured, but Fischer didn't know that. I hoisted up on my elbows and began dragging myself toward the pit. I didn't even have to get all the way there to make this work. Just a little closer.

"I have something for you." Fischer reached into his own pocket and removed a piece of paper. I knew exactly what it was.

"I don't care," I said.

"You should."

"You drugged me."

"You needed help getting free from your mental prison."

"You're probably right," I said, commando crawling, elbows and legs working together.

Fischer held the paper toward me.

I took it, looked at it, tossed it aside.

"So what?" I said.

"God will forgive you."

"Oh, yeah? Do I get a cross branded on my chest if He says 'Sure thing, Rowe'?"

"You can't run from it." Fischer took in the scene without concern. People were calming down. Some were gathered around Brock and someone else was helping Melissa to her feet. "'For God shall bring every work into judgement, with every secret thing, whether it be good, or whether it be evil.' Your pain, your sins, your evil, they can all be burned away. Nothing is more powerful than God's holy fire."

"Funny you should say that," I said.

Fischer stared down at me. "Leave us," he said. "Please. We don't deserve any of this."

"Sure you do," I said.

"Why?"

"Because there's still one more fire to burn."

In my hand was the bright yellow pocket lighter I'd bought at the gas station, along with the gas (both for my truck and to fill the two five-gallon containers that I'd dumped on the fire pit and all over the ground.) My thumb rolled on the flint wheel and a long flame appeared.

Fischer's confusion became shock and fear when I launched off the ground and ran the rest of the way to the fire pit.

The flame blew out, of course, but I flicked the lighter again and brought fire to a heavily soaked branch. *Fffooomp!* Flames slipped all along the stacked wood, crisscrossing through the pile, slicking around it to the teepee top and stretching toward the sky.

But that wasn't all.

Fire caught the gasoline trail I'd left. Quick as a fired bullet, the flames raced across the ground. They reached the cabin and flexed along the outside wall. I'd splashed gasoline all along that wall and pooled it thick on the ground.

Flames pushed waist- and then shoulder-high and were then well over six-foot tall and growing.

Burn, motherfucker, burn, I thought, which was something Petey used to say whenever the troops were given cleanup duty because that meant we could use a burn barrel.

People were running again, screaming, women hoisting children onto their hips and staggering from the fire. Men yelling commands. One man slung off his shirt and beat at the flames. Another woman stopped mid-run, grabbing at her side, and fell to one knee and then fell over. A little girl with tangled brown hair watched this, her thumb filling her mouth. Someone else snatched the girl by the arm and yanked her into the air.

They were running everywhere, scattering into the woods in all directions.

But not Fischer.

He stood with his son hugged to his side and watched as what he had built burned. As his followers fled.

Black smoke coiled into the sky.

I walked back to him. The fire was hot at my back.

"What was it you said, God baptizes with fire?"

He wasn't really seeing me. His gaze was the thousand-mile stare of the traumatized.

He opened his mouth and—

The rolling, ululating, howling wail of a fire engine's siren filled the air. It was deafening. Because the truck was very close.

Trees fell in snapping pops, and the woods itself pulled back as a dump truck emerged right by the cabin that was quickly charring, the flames now on the roof. The truck was yellow and black like the toy Tonka versions of it kids played with. Branches and bushes and twigs tangled in the enormous front grille.

The truck rumbled in farther. A woman in shorts, it might've been Pash, raised her hands to stop it but the truck kept coming and she sprinted out of the way.

Good thing because right behind the truck rumbled in the fire engine.

Fire Chief Graham and some other locals, like the guy who worked for the local DPW and who was manning the dump truck, had been forging the path I followed through the woods for weeks now. The dump truck and fire engine really didn't have to make it through too much. All they needed was an excuse to come back here. *A really big damn fire would do it,* Graham told me.

"What have you done?" Fischer said.

"It is God's will," I said. "Now, give me your kid."

I didn't even have to put the gun on him. Fischer set his son down on his feet and stepped back.

Men and women half-dressed in fire-fighting gear unloaded from the truck and gathered at the front. Chief Graham stood in the middle, rubbing at his mustache.

Behind the truck, an ambulance pulled up. Good thing. Brock might be bleeding out.

The sirens competed with the screams of people running and the roar of fire beginning to really eat up the place.

Graham and his people watched it happen.

Burn, motherfucker, burn.

I waved for the pair of paramedics to come over and they hurried, red duffel bags in hand, blue windbreakers flapping like capes.

Fischer was gone.

The kid tugged my hand.

I knelt before him. Should I hug him, tell him he was safe? I suddenly felt completely ill equipped to do for this kid what should come naturally.

"Landon." Melissa stood over me. Sweat dotted her forehead. "I need to get my son back."

43

The plan worked, you could say, but I hadn't expected to be back in my truck headed to Father Benny's with my ex-wife in the passenger seat. Hadn't expected to shoot Brock, either.

Life is full of surprises.

This may sound heartless, I guess, but I left Fischer's son with Graham. The kid didn't seem to mind, his hand resting on the side of the fire engine and his eyes going big with wonder instead of fear.

"What's his name?" Graham asked.

"Isaac," I said.

The kid didn't respond. Firelight flickered on his face.

Graham's people finally started unspooling a fire hose. Directly over the cabin, leaves were singeing and bark was burning. The smoke was getting thicker and blacker. Even so, Graham's people were in no rush.

"Controlled burn," Graham said.

I knelt before the kid again. "I'm sorry all this happened to you," I said. "You'll be okay."

He would end up in some foster home somewhere, but I had to believe that was better than being with Fischer and his Fire Gospel. Only a matter of time before Fischer branded the kid's chest with a cross.

I know what you're thinking—I could raise the kid. Go through the foster parenting process, adoption, etc. Flash forward to months, even years later, and there's Landon Rowe playing Daddy for a kid who desperately needed a father.

You can pretend that's what happens, if you want, but real life doesn't work that way.

"Stay strong, kid," I said.

Mel didn't say anything for almost an hour. Traffic was light and we were making great time.

"I'm sorry," she said. I glanced at her reflection in the passenger window. She had that far-off, longing look that she always got just before packing a bag for another soul quest.

"We're going to get your son back." I pictured Father Benny opening his front door, face mask with a cross on it drooping, over-starched shirt and baggy khakis, and bare feet, of course. The damn kid was there the whole time and I never suspected. *If criminals weren't so stupid, being a cop would be a hell of a lot harder.* "We're getting Eli."

Melissa sighed, faced me but I didn't look at her. Before

she could speak, I said, "Why didn't you leave him with your mother?"

"Landon—"

"You could've dropped him on her front porch. Hell, you could've left him with me."

"Landon."

"Or are you sorry for cheating on me? Sorry for getting pregnant with Brock's kid?"

"Landon."

"What?"

"I'm sorry for *our* son. It was my fault. I don't say that easily or with any relief. I say it because it's true. I left that stupid blanket on the heater. I killed our son."

Squeezing the steering wheel and clenching my jaw kept the tears from falling. My eyes burned with the effort.

"You don't have to say anything," Mel said. "I'm only telling you this because it's taken me a long time to admit it to myself. I didn't want to. I wanted to blame you. Or God. Especially God. Why did my son have to die when there's cruel, evil people all over the world who keep right on living? That doesn't sound fair. It sounds fucked up."

It sounds like there is no God, I thought.

"I hate myself, Landon. If I wasn't such a coward, I would've swallowed a bottle of pills or taken a razor blade to my wrist." She was speaking calmly but the threat of tears threaded her words. "I've worked really hard just so I can say *that*. I don't know if it's God or what, but I *am* getting better."

"Yeah," I said through my teeth. "That's why you left your kid with a religious psycho."

She didn't say anything else.

44

We made it to Father Reed's before noon.

We parked at the curb. The brown ranch-style house was quiet. Now instead of the bushes out front looking lazily unkempt, they looked purposefully overgrown. It's what you did when you didn't want people peering in your windows but you didn't want to create suspicion by having your curtains closed all the time.

"I'll go," Mel said. "I dropped him off here. Now, I'm picking him up."

"Give me my tool bag," I said.

She had to try twice to get a good enough grip to lift it. "What's in this thing?"

I took it, searched, found what I wanted.

"What're you doing with that?"

I worked the utility knife button to slide the razor blade into cutting position. It wasn't a hammer, but it would work.

"Whatever I need to," I said.

"You really think he did something?" She was taking rapid shallow breaths.

"When was he expecting you to come back?"

She had to focus hard to speak. "Call the police."

I grabbed the door handle. "We could, and we can wait for them, assuming they believe us, and eventually they'll get here, but in the meantime your son is still inside and—"

"Let's go."

45

You might think I'd have to break down the door or that I needed to sneak around back and see if there was a way into the basement, but Father Reed didn't know what was coming. Even the guilty who know they deserve the worst of what could be coming, never think that justice is right now when someone is casually knocking at the door.

He opened the door wearing a yellow button-down, a cross stitched on the breast pocket, baggy khakis, and a black face mask with a gold cross on it. Bare feet too, of course.

"Told you I'd be seeing you, Benny Boy."

"Landon? Melissa?"

"Oh, good, you remember. Where's Eli?"

"Eli?"

"Oh, don't remember him?"

"My son!" Melissa said. "Give me my son!"

Benny fumbled something close to words but he was

trying to distract me as he adjusted his grip on the door, readying to slam it.

One of my boots (courtesy of Chief Graham) thunked across the doorway, almost catching his toes. "We're coming in, Benny Boy."

He yammered excuses I neither heard nor cared about.

I yanked the mask off his face, tossed it aside.

"Move," I said.

"No," he said. "You can't!" His face blushed crimson starbursts. His skin was slick, almost slimy. "I'm not done! I need more time! *You weren't supposed to be back!"*

Lucky for him, the utility knife was in my pocket. If it'd been in my hand, things could've gotten messy. I grabbed handfuls of his starched shirt and drove him several backpedaling steps into his house before letting him go with one final shove. He hit the floor with a heavy thump and a pained cry.

"Where's the basement?"

"I... I... You can't. *You can't!"*

Melissa made as if to kick him, perhaps even in the head, but then she changed her mind and hurried past me and rushed down the hall.

Benny was starting to get up but I shoved a knee against his chest and from my pocket I removed not the knife but something else I'd grabbed from my tool bag—thick plastic tie wraps.

He resisted but couldn't do much. I cinched his wrists together behind his back, pulling the ties tight enough to cut off blood flow, and then I did his ankles. He was making a crying, groaning kind of sound.

"Don't go anywhere," I said.

"You can't," he said. "I'm not done. *He isn't purified yet!*"

Mel was calling for me and banging on a door.

I hurried, passing several crucifixes on the wall. Had there been this many when I was last here and I didn't notice?

"This is the basement," she said. "It's locked."

Not much space to get leverage, but I grabbed the knob and flung my shoulder into the door. The lock popped and I almost stumbled down the steps.

Mel descended.

Smelled like something was burning down there.

I was right behind her.

"No!" Benny was yelling. *"He's not purified!"*

The basement was small and the white sheets hanging on the walls with giant gold crosses on them made it claustrophobic. There was a mini altar with a kneeler before it and a life-sized crucified Jesus behind that.

The perfect prayer basement—for a psycho.

Near the altar was a camping propane stove. Smoke was curling off the cast iron pan in which simmered a long-handled fireplace tool.

Not a tool. A branding iron.

You've smelled it before—the stink of burning meat—but you never smelled anything like this.

Mel made a sound that was somewhere between a terrified scream and a cat's quavering yowl.

Her son, Eli, was on a soiled mat on the concrete floor, dressed only in his underwear. It's hard to say what I noticed first because he was so badly damaged. His skin was deeply charred in places and swollen in purple-brown welts and oily slicked. There seemed no part of his body untouched. His face too was a horror—bulged and bleeding, blood like lava in charred earth.

He could only open one eye.

In that single-eyed stare, he pleaded not for help or vengeance but death.

I will never forget that.

Mel made that awful sound again and collapsed by her child. She wanted to take him in her arms but she couldn't see a place to touch him without hurting.

I yanked a sheet off the wall and we carefully wrapped him in it. He was shaking and crying. A cross was singed into his forehead.

We are all children of fire.

God has a plan for each of us. There are demands set upon each soul. Sacrifices to be made. The crosses we carry can be very heavy.

Mel cradled her wrapped child and rocked with him, her

pained cry so like the one she voiced when I was giving our baby CPR on the kitchen counter.

Inside me, I felt a thing like a board creaking under pressure.

I hurried back upstairs.

Father Reed glared up at me.

"You fucking degenerate," I said.

He opened his mouth but I moved fast, getting down, and wedging the sharp utility blade into the dangly flap of his neck.

When I was here last he'd asked if I wanted to pray with him, to go downstairs to his "home church." *God's will,* he probably told himself.

Instead, it was no different than a serial killer inviting the police in to look around.

"You deserve to die."

I could stab him. *Should* stab him. Or at least carve something into *his* flesh. Sicko, maybe, or Sinner.

I pressed down, pinching and puncturing his skin in a dimple of blood.

Letting your feelings cloud your judgement.

"Jesus said, 'Allow the children to come to me.'" Benny's voice was shaking, his eyes huge. "'For the kingdom of heaven is theirs.'"

Please, God, I wanted to gut him.

I leaned close.

Blood trailed down his neck to wet his collar.

Do it, my inner voice said. *Why not? You've already done more than enough to deserve a prison sentence. You might as well really make it worth it. Kill this warped man, this so-called priest, this child abuser. Kill him and make your dead son proud!*

My hand, my arm, my whole body was completely rigid.

I pressed the blade in farther. More blood.

Tremors shook him and he closed his eyes and whispered some prayer to his god, the same god for whom he'd tortured a child.

Send him to his god if that's what he wants so badly. Be the avenging angel. Kill him.

My face to his face. I smelled the odor of his fear.

"Please..."

Kill him. Do it.

I snorted, breathing hard through my nose. Oinking.

"Whoink!"

Good as detonating a flashbang. Benny blinked repeatedly, stunned.

I punched him—*hard.*

Knocked him out.

Then I called 9-1-1.

Outside on the porch, I felt better. The day was warming but the humidity was lifting.

After I lit a Marlboro, I felt better yet.

Smoking was always good for filling life's pauses.

46

If I had to guess, I'd say doctors are taught in medical school to never tell patients and their families exactly what is wrong with them or exactly how a procedure will turn out. There must be a class in using ambiguous, noncommittal phrasing, and extra credit if you can conceal your meaning in metaphor. He's doing well but we're not out of the woods yet. We can be cautiously optimistic. He's a fighter and that's what matters. We're doing everything we can.

What do you say about a four-year-old whose chest and back have been seared like meat on a grill?

Mel spends all day at the hospital and sleeps in a waiting room most nights. Eli's in the burn ward so she can't sleep by his bedside.

When she goes home, it's to my place not hers.

Brock was only in the hospital two days. He's living in the house, my old house. He shouldn't be there. It's a bad place. Maybe Brock is a bad man. Maybe that's the pot calling the kettle black. When he visits Eli, Mel goes in with him. She's not hiding from him anymore.

She filed for divorce.

The anniversary of our son's death came and went.

I got drunk every night and fell asleep on the couch with Sherman curled on my chest. I'd wake with a pounding headache and a sour slick in my throat. That wasn't bad really. Except after the second cup of black coffee when the hangover fog started to lift, I felt the anger creeping back. It curls my fingers into fists, and vibrates up along my arms and cuts through my face the way a knife carves up a pumpkin.

The drinking helps.

So, I had a choice: keep drinking or do something about the anger.

The conversation was quick. I stopped Mel before she headed back toward the burn ward.

"I'm leaving. I may be gone a while."

"Why?"

"Because if I stay, I might do something bad."

I didn't want to tell her about the nightmares in which her son is forever opening that one eye, begging for death, and the air is thick with the stink of burned flesh. And then Eli is Ethan. I handed her my key to the apartment.

"Don't forget about Sherman."

Mel will be okay. She has Eli. That's her purpose now. Her soul quest is his well being.

I kissed her right on the lips but it was passionless, a kiss a priest might bestow upon a man about to walk his final steps to his execution. Except of course, I was the one making the walk.

47

Minnewaska is a state park in Kerhonkson. You get there taking 44/55, cutting through Gardiner until it's just you, the road, and the mountain. You pass the Brauhaus (excellent sauerbraten) and the Mohonk Mountain House is nearby (rumor has it, it's haunted), but you follow the mountain up, up, up and there's a damn good lookout over the valley even if you never get out of your car.

It's busy most days during the summer and especially on the weekend. I went late on a Tuesday, the sun into its slow summery descent, but there were still plenty of casual wanderers in flips and yoga pants with phones in hand to document every potential pretty picture as well as the more serious-minded hikers in Patagonia gear with matching backpack, bear bells dangling off the zippers, hiking poles in hand.

I wore my usual—work shirt, jeans, and (a new pair) of Red Wings. I also threw on a Red Sox cap that looked splashed with oil. A pair of teenage girls gave me suspicious glares as if I were, to use their lingo, creeping on them, but most people ignored me.

I moved casually, taking in the woods and the beautiful lake, but I was searching. You could say it was a quest. He was around here somewhere. I was sure of it.

It would be too convenient for him to be at Gertrude's Nose, where he was on that video Benny showed me, but I went there anyway. A couple was sitting crosslegged on the slab of rock that juts out toward the lake. The sun was a starburst about to slip behind the distant mountain and the lake mirrored the purplish rose of the sky. Would've been a good picture. I left my phone in the truck. Along with my gun and all my tools.

"It's beautiful, isn't it?"

Fischer had found me.

I didn't turn around.

"There's no way you can look at that, a thing so magnificently beautiful, and not believe in God. It's like looking into the infinity of God's mind," Fischer said.

I turned to face him. "It's pretty enough for a postcard," I said.

Without any bandana on his head, his grey hair dangled everywhere. He slipped it behind both ears but it wouldn't stay. It pooled on his shoulders, and I wanted to grab a handful of it and yank it right out of his scalp. I could bring it to Eli as proof I'd hurt the man who had created the monster who hurt him. In only the few weeks since I'd last seen him, Fischer aged another decade and lost another ten pounds, maybe fifteen.

He was, of course, barefoot.

"How is Isaac?" he asked.

"You abandoned him."

He thought about that, staring at me unblinking, the setting light shining right into his eyes. "He would've been taken from me."

"God took my kid," I said. "But if I could've grabbed him right from God's greedy hands I would have. I would have made God strike me dead before I'd let my child be taken."

Neither of us said anything for a long time.

If there were loons on the lake, it would've been the perfect moment for them to make their lamenting cry. Instead, I caught a bit of passing conversational debate about what toppings a family was going to order on a pizza and the young woman behind me on the rock made an "ohh-ahh" sound as if she were watching fireworks. I heard the soft press of her lips against the young man's beside her.

"Melissa's son?" Fischer asked.

"His name is Eli. He's alive but he's in a lot of pain. Severe burns."

Fischer whispered a prayer.

"Cut the shit, Fischer."

He did.

"If you're here to kill me," he said. "Just do it."

I chuckled. I wanted to be angry, hell, I *was* angry, but I wasn't here to attack him, not here to hurt him. I'd hurt enough people.

"Why *are* you here?" he asked.

Usually, I know what I'm going to say. Not this time.

"I wish I'd killed Benny. I want that moment back. When I saw what he did to that little boy. I want that back. Why didn't I do it? Why didn't I beat him or burn him or cut him or shoot him? Did God stay my hand like that angel stopping Abraham from killing his son? Why would God protect such a cruel man?"

"You want me to answer that?" Fischer asked. He sounded quite sad. Defeated.

"Someone should."

Again, neither of us said anything for a long, long time.

The couple got up and walked past us. The woman pointed at Fischer's feet and whispered, "He's earthing."

I took out my pocket ledger, opened to the page on which Fischer had written, *God forgives you*, and removed a folded piece of paper.

He was staring at me—but finally he blinked.

"It's true," I said. My voice was a rope pulled taut. "What I wrote on this paper: I killed my son."

If I was going to hit him, it would've been right then.

And if I'd started hitting him, I don't know how I would've stopped. But as I said, I'd hurt enough people.

My knees gave out and I fell.

Somewhere inside me, that creaking-board-under-pressure snapped.

The tears were already falling from my eyes but there was so much more, an ocean of it, and I let it flood free. Sobs punched my body. It was guilt. Mel and I were drunk and had sex and we were so tired because Ethan could cry for hours and hours and nothing placated him, but he was finally, mercifully, asleep. *I'll check on him,* I told myself, maybe even mumbled it aloud. But I didn't. And that's how it happens. How a child dies.

"It's my fault," I said, my body shaking and crumbling beneath a barrage of invisible assailants. *"Oh, God, it's my fault."*

Fischer didn't say anything until my shaking eased and my tears let up enough for me to wipe at them with my palms.

"Why are you here, Landon?"

"I don't want to feel like this anymore."

He got to his knees in front of me. The lake was behind us and the sun was shedding the last splash of its ethereal colors before dropping behind a mountain. An everyday occurrence, yet one that might be proof of God's infinite mind.

Fischer touched my arm. "Would you like to pray with me?"

48

I used to think being a cop and a detective gave my life purpose.

I came to believe that no matter what good you managed, there was so much awful shit that a little bit of good didn't matter. Nothing mattered. Good cop. Bad cop. Straightedge or corrupt. Doesn't make a difference.

When my son died, I knew it for fact: the universe is indifferent. Or maybe it's even cruel. Kids die. Or get burned so badly death would be better.

Life goes on.

There's no more Children of Fire, no cult, no followers, only Fischer and me.

I don't know if I can find meaning or peace. Or if it even matters.

I don't know if this is a soul quest or a waste of time.

I don't care if the Hudson Valley is the new Holy Land or just another pretty place.

I don't know what I want.

We've been in the woods for a week now. They towed my truck. The park closes at seven but Fischer knows how to get around without being detected. He knows what's edible, and what might make you hallucinate.

Fischer was right about the feet. After a few days of bleeding, my soles thickened into calluses that get meatier every day.

We're dirty and hungry.

We burn a fire at night. I stare at it for hours. Is it true God spoke through a burning bush? That He created a pillar of fire to lead the Jews out of exile?

Doesn't matter.

Because maybe there *is* no meaning to anything.

Fischer and I talk about that often. Mostly, though, we sit in silence with the trees around us and the lake before us reflecting the sky, and we pray.

God hasn't answered me yet.

But I keep praying.

Maybe that's enough.

AUTHOR'S NOTE
& ACKNOWLEDGEMENTS

I'd wanted to write this story for years.

In the first decade of this century, I saw *Gone Baby Gone*, *Prisoners*, and the first season of *True Detective* one right after the other. I was enamored with each.

I wanted to write my own story that would have a similar feel.

My first attempt was *Dark Heart*, a thriller about a newly widowed woman who discovers her husband's secret life. Although I admired that woman, Brielle Heart, it was James Hunter, the former FBI serial killer profiler who helps Bri unravel the mystery, who I really loved. I wanted more stories with him.

Maybe one day I will write those stories.

I also tried my hand at two screenplays. One was about a detective investigating a series of grisly child murders in the Hudson Valley. *Dark Valley*, I titled it. The other was about a husband-and-wife detective duo who, still grieving over the loss of their own child, confront a religious cult whose leader convinces parents to set their children on fire. This one was called *The Fire Gospel*. I still like that idea.

My writing process is disciplined and mechanical yet also scattershot and unwieldy and very often a complete mystery. Whatever it was that carried those two stories from inspiration to written word petered out and neither of those scripts made it very far, but the ideas in them continued to simmer in my imagination.

At some point, I wrote the following line: *There's always smoke even when there isn't fire.* What followed was a page or so of semi-hallucinatory imagery in which a father is continually suffering nightmares of how his infant child succumbed to smoke inhalation.

I wrote it, liked it, and had no idea where to go next and so I set it aside.

Over a decade after attempting to write those original scripts, another sentence came to me. *I used to think being a cop and a detective gave my life purpose.* The voice intrigued me, and I hand wrote eight pages, Palomino Blackwing pencil on yellow Bloc Rhoda N°19.

I was chasing that voice, Landon Rowe's voice, and what I found was an entire story.

Those handwritten pages became the opening of this book.

Halfway through that sequence with Rowe and Brock, I

jumped from paper to computer. I knew what was at stake, and I knew what my character had to do, and what lesson he was bound to learn.

I also found a place for that earlier line about smoke—it starts off Chapter 23.

In any crime novel, the detective has a job to do, and he or she has to investigate and interrogate. This sets up scenes in a way that is propulsive for the reader and reassuring for the writer. When the scenes start stacking up, one clearly leading to the next and the next and so on, pages accumulate and the writer is never so happy.

That's how it was with *Children of Fire*.

I had a blast writing this story and when, at the midpoint, I saw what was *really* going on, I jumped out of my chair with glee. Then I sat back down and wrote as fast as I could. In two months, I had a complete draft.

I really love this story.

It's Rowe's voice, I think, that makes me so fond of this story—it strikes me as true. He's trying to do what's right and he's struggling with his personal demons. He's angry at the world. He wields sarcasm as a shield and a sword. I can relate. To some extent, the characters that writers create are a reflection of those writers. Or maybe that sounds too pompous, too full-of-itself literary? So be it. I dig this story and I hope you did too.

Immense thanks to D. Alexander Ward and Gina

Scapellato at Bleeding Edge Books for believing in this story. I'm thrilled to publish with them. David and Gina helped improve this story, and I'm immensely grateful. Thanks to Don Noble for his awesome cover and Todd Keisling for the internal layout. Thanks to Michael Marshall and Michael Koryta, both masterful writers who have given of their time to lend advice and offer generous encouragement. Thanks to Tim Waggoner, whose book *Writing in the Dark* gave me the perfect approach to crafting a crucial sequence in this story.

Thank you to my wife, Jenn, for her unwavering belief and support.

And thank you, dear reader, for giving this book a chance. I hope you made it through without getting burned too badly.

I wish you well.

Chris DiLeo
June 2022

ABOUT THE AUTHOR

Chris DiLeo is the author of eight other books, including *Dead End* from JournalStone and *Revival Road* from Bloodshot Books. He is a high school English teacher in New York. The above photo was taken by his wife, Jenn, and shows him before his *Boys Can Read Too* collection. Connect with him @authordileo.

www.ingramcontent.com/pod-product-compliance
Lightning Source LLC
LaVergne TN
LVHW041800060526
838201LV00046B/1073